BROKEN
ONES

by

SARAH A. DENZIL

PROLOGUE

One. Two. Now you. One. Two. Now you.

The garden smells nice. Warm leaves. Warmth underfoot. Sun overhead. *Count the birds.* One. Two. Three. Magpies, all of them. Black, blue, and white. They sound funny—scratchy and coarse—when they sing. I don't like that sound. It frightens me. Maybe I should go inside? I don't want to. I want to feel the sunshine on my skin. When I close my eyes, the afterimage of the sun is bright red, like the blood that came out when I scraped my knee last year.

One. Two.

What comes next? What did we do?

Now you.

I don't remember what comes next. Why am I forgetting?

"What are you doing out here?"

I tense at the sound of her voice. It's high-pitched and urgent. That means she's mad about something. Her footsteps hurry over. Then her cold hand grasps my arm.

"We don't have time for this. You need to get ready," she says.

"I don't want to," I whisper. I always whisper when I disobey her. It's the only way I dare to do it.

She yanks me, and I cry out. Her fingernails dig into my skin and tears wet my cheeks.

"I told you not to play out here," she says. She's sweating. Her hair has come loose from her hairdo, and the straggles stick to her forehead. Her blouse is stained and unbuttoned at the top. Her eyes are ringed with dark circles, and her lipstick is smudged. But still, she's terrifying to me. Still, she drags me across the grass. "What are you doing out here, anyway? Who were you talking to?"

I don't want to say.

"Well?" she insists. Her nails dig harder into my skin.

"The shadow," I whisper.

She stops. I'm afraid now. Afraid of the silence that follows. She sinks down to my height, and all I can think about are her bloodshot eyes, how frantic they are.

"There is no shadow," she says. "There never was a shadow. You need to stop this nonsense right now."

I nod my head. I will. I will stop this nonsense. I promise.

I just want her to love me.

PART ONE

CHAPTER ONE

My name is Sophie Howland, and, never—not even for one single moment in my sorry existence—have I ever felt like a whole person. There's a part of me that's missing. It's as though a dog tore away a piece of me shortly after I was born. I got eaten all up, like leftovers.

Now that I'm older, I believe that missing piece might one day be filled in by having a family. You see, I've always wanted children. I want, more than anything, to belong to a clan. To have it all: husband… kids… the lot. Mum raised me on her own after Dad died, so I wanted a taste of the normal nuclear life. Perhaps the stars didn't align for me and it was never part of my destiny. Perhaps, at thirty-five, I will be a late bloomer. Everything will click for me all of a sudden. You hear of that happening to women. They're usually rich or famous women over forty, settling down after a glittering career, able to afford a surrogate, not a primary school teacher living with her mother in a small English town.

Despite my not finding a husband, you could say that I have the child. I have a fifty-five-year-old, stubborn, angry, confused child. But this child isn't going to grow up. It's going to become a baby. As Mum's mind disintegrates, she's going to lose a lot of functionality. Soon I'll have to feed, bathe, and dress her, like a baby. She is slowly becoming my baby. The one I never had.

I still remember being in the doctor's surgery as our GP delivered the news. I remember how the room narrowed and the light winnowed to spotlight the bald, shiny head of Dr. Lee. I remember the pencil that rolled slowly across the desk, and the dirty coffee mug sitting on an old coaster. I remember how the words decelerated and distorted, then sped up without warning. Early. Onset. Alzheimer's. And then a thought popped into my mind: *This is my punishment.* Because I knew I'd have to care for her. There was no one else to do it. This is my punishment for never being the daughter I was supposed to be. And there's nothing I can do about it. All I can do is watch her as her mind is slowly eaten away by the disease.

Since then, I've lived only half for myself. My first thoughts are always of her; she has to come first, now that she's vulnerable. I'm in a constant push and pull with myself, a tug of war about how

I will live my life. I have friends who pull me one way, while I push myself in another direction, striving for a life I'll probably never get. Then there is that perpetual pull from Mum. The constant need. Continually, I ask myself, should I stop living for her? Should I give everything up: my dreams of a normal life with a husband and family? I know what Mum would want. I know what she would say. Maybe I've made the wrong decision. I don't know.

I arrive at the café early. I knew I would. I worked out that it would take me twenty minutes to walk, but then I decided to give myself an extra ten minutes "just in case". Before I knew it, I'd talked myself into leaving an hour early. But that's okay. I can sit here and read my book, enjoying the sound of the coffee machine and ridding myself of the stresses at home.

I check my phone again, reminding myself of what he looks like, then I glance at the door to the café. He won't be here yet; there's still forty-five minutes to go until the time we agreed to meet. It's 11am on Saturday, and the only other people in here are couples having brunch together, and a few people with their laptops, sipping cappuccinos. Even though it seems fairly unlikely that my internet date will murder me at 11am on a Saturday in broad daylight, Mum still tried to talk me out of going. Luckily, she lost her keys and got distracted, meaning I could slip out unnoticed, leaving her with Erin, her nurse.

7

I stir my coffee. It's not good for me to think about Mum all day, which is what I usually do. Like the doctor keeps telling me, worrying about it isn't going to cure her Alzheimer's, but it might make me ill too. She has Erin. She's fine.

Even though she's been deteriorating quickly — as people with early onset Alzheimer's tend to do — she was still aware enough to tell me that wearing my hair up only makes my slightly-too-large jaw look even bigger, and that my cardigan is frumpy. How do mothers do that? How do they always manage to slip in a criticism as easily as saying hello? It seems to be second nature.

The door opens, and my head snaps up. This is him. He's shorter than I thought he would be. The photograph on his profile must be a few years old — or was taken in very good light — because it doesn't show the wrinkles around his eyes and the grey in his beard. But he has a nice smile. He clocks me right away and walks over with his head bent low, staring at his feet. I can't help but notice his shoes. They're some sort of work boot, scuffed as though he's been wearing them every day for years. The rest of his outfit is jeans and a zip-up top.

"You must be Sophie," he says. "I'm Peter."

I shake his hand and then try to discretely wipe his sweat on my skirt. "Hi, Peter. It's nice to meet you."

He sits down and shuffles the chair towards the table. His large stomach presses against the lip of the table. "You look just like your picture," he says.

I'm not sure whether to take that as a compliment or not.

"What are you drinking?" he asks.

"Oh, an Americana."

"I don't like coffee myself," he says. "The caffeine makes me jittery. My mum never let me drink tea when I was a child. It's probably because of that."

Mentioning Mum in the first minute… could be a bad sign. Then again, maybe we'll bond over our dysfunctional maternal relationships. Seeing as it was my dysfunctional maternal relationship that destroyed my last romance, that might help.

"So, you're an accountant?" I ask.

"Yes," he says. "It's a small firm, but we have loyal clients. We get enough work to keep us going. It's mostly self-employed people. You'd be amazed at how unorganised they are." He laughs. "Last year I got a bunch of receipts in a plastic bag."

I raise my eyebrows. "Oh, that sounds —"

Luckily, the waitress comes over to take Peter's order, saving me from trying to make more conversation. I'm not quite sure what to say next.

"What is it that you're reading?" Peter gestures to the upside down book on the table.

"Oh." I turn it over. "*Jane Eyre*. It's my third read-through. I tend to read it every five years or so, to remind myself of why I love it."

Peter laughs at this. It's like a big "Ha!" Then he says, "I don't like to read. I'd rather play video games. Don't you think it's exhausting, trying to imagine all those characters? And writers, well. They're all narcissists."

"How so?" I ask.

"Who else would sit there on their own and imagine people having a conversation? It's weird."

The waitress brings Peter a Coke. He slurps half of it down.

I'm still floored by his last comments. "But don't you think that people need stories? And that our language is beautiful?"

He narrows his eyes. "You're an English teacher, aren't you?"

I bristle. "No. A primary school teacher. But I studied English at university."

He clicks his fingers and grins. "I knew it!"

I grit my teeth, choosing not to remind him that my occupation was listed on my dating profile. Maybe if I can get him off the topic of English literature, he'll show some hidden depths. "What are your interests, Peter? Do you like music?" Everyone likes music.

"More arrogant twats," he says. "I can't stand rock stars, can you? Knobheads like Bono trying to save the world."

I shuffle my weight, physically cringing away from his penetrating gaze. I hate how confrontational he is. It's as though everything he says has to be a debate. This isn't a good start. Right now, I just want to leave. Being at home with my ill mother is preferable to this. "I suppose so.

What about classical music, then?"

"I don't have the patience for it. Now, country and western, that's all right. Kenny Rogers, Dolly Parton. She wrote 'I Will Always Love You'. The original. Then Shitney Houston ruined it." He laughs at his own joke.

I'm nodding along when my phone rings. "I'm really sorry—I should take this. My mother hasn't been well."

"Of course," he says, and I can't help but notice how his eyes light up at the mention of my mother.

I'm both relieved to get the call at such an opportune moment, and heart-heavy for how the date is going, plus there's the prospect of problems at home. I find a quiet corner of the café and swipe my finger across the screen to accept the call.

"Erin, what's wrong?" I ask, immediately anxious.

"It's nothing to be *too* concerned about," she says in a voice an octave higher than usual. I can picture her standing by the kitchen work surface, her arms flapping up and down as she speaks. Erin is a decade younger than I am, and sometimes her energy makes me feel exhausted. "But Mum isn't doing too good today." She always talks about Mum as though she's a child. That doesn't bother me so much. Mum is so awful to her that I allow Erin any little eccentricity she likes to make the job easier. "She's quite agitated. She keeps asking for you. I'm so sorry to interrupt your date—"

"No, that's okay," I jump in. "To tell you the

truth, I was looking for an excuse to leave."

"That bad, huh?" Erin asks.

I glance across at Peter, who waves enthusiastically. I arrange my face into an expression I hope shows concern but not distress, and then shrug my shoulders apologetically.

"Yeah. He seems nice, but..."

"Not your cup of tea?" she finishes.

I sigh. "Not really. I'll be home in twenty minutes."

I hang up the phone and head back to Peter, sat slurping on his Coke. When he places the glass back down, there's still moisture on his moustache, which makes me feel a little queasy.

"I'm sorry, Peter, but I'll have to go. My mother is suffering with early onset Alzheimer's disease, and the nurse has phoned to tell me that she's very distressed. I'm going to have to go home."

"Oh, what a shame," he says. He finally wipes his mouth and frowns. "Can I drive you home?"

"That's all right. I only live a few minutes away," I lie. I don't want to be alone with him in a moving vehicle.

"I could walk you home." He smiles. It *is* a nice smile. There's every chance that he's a nice man, just not very good with people.

"No, you stay and finish your drink. I must hurry. It was very nice to meet you."

The waitress winks at me as I hurry out of the café. I almost laugh, but then I think about going home, and the laugh fizzles out before it can begin.

*

"I will not do that."

My shoulders are heavier when I hear her voice. Loud, cockney, mean-spirited. Three words my mother has embodied for my entire life.

"Get off me!"

"Mrs. Howland, please. You need to eat something."

I open the door as a smash of china rings out through the house. "Mum? What are you doing?" I hurry into the kitchen to see a broken bowl sitting in a puddle of soup on the kitchen floor. "Why did you do that, Mum?"

"This woman broke into my house and tried to feed me poison," she says with her nose in the air. Mum always stands tall and proud. She's thin as a rake, with eyes as sharp as an eagle's. It's only her mind that has lost its edge.

"Mum, that's Erin. She looks after you." I smile at Erin, who's paid for in part by the Alzheimer's charity. She's a sweet twenty-something with a pixie hairdo and a nose ring. "Come on, sit down for a moment. I'll get this cleared up." I try to herd her towards the dining table, but she bats my hand away.

"I can't sit down, you stupid bitch. I've lost my keys."

Erin's eyes widen at the language, but I don't even flinch.

"I've got your keys, Mum. They're in my bag. I'll give them to you after you've eaten."

Lying to Mum got a lot easier when she started forgetting things every five minutes. But when her eyes narrow, I know I'm in trouble. When her eyes flash, and she goes quieter, I know she's having one of her more lucid moments. "So, how was it, then? I see you kept your hair like that, even though I said not to."

Erin bends down to help me pick up the pieces of broken bowl. When I stand, I avoid eye contact with my mother. It's in these moments that I feel like a ten-year-old child, not a thirty-five-year-old woman.

"He was nice," I say. "But I don't think we'll see each other again."

She laughs. "Not with that jaw." She turns to Erin, who she's evidently decided is not a murdering burglar anymore. "You should've seen her as a baby. Chin like an anvil." She tips her head back and laughs. "I didn't know whether to feed her or hammer a horseshoe on her." She laughs again.

Erin flashes me a pitying smile. She opens a bin bag, and we drop the pieces of the bowl into it.

"Still, at least he didn't rape and murder you," Mum continues. "That's what happens on these internet dates. They're all perverts. He probably grooms teenagers in his spare time. I bet that's why he didn't bother. You're too long in the tooth."

"Mum," I say. My voice is quiet. Too quiet to

stop my mother. I move across the kitchen to get a rag to clean up the spilled soup. Erin is silent. My insides crawl with embarrassment. I hate it when others witness what she's like.

"I told you not to go, didn't I?" Her green eyes bore into mine. When I was little, I thought lasers would come out of them, as if she were an evil superman.

"You did," I say.

"And I was right, wasn't I?" she says.

"Yes," I reply.

"I'm always right." She moves a few strands of her hair back. She likes to have it set just so. Many hairdressers have been screamed at. "Aren't I?"

"Yes." I wring out the rag in the kitchen sink and try not to say anything more. Erin starts on another batch of soup.

"Did I tell you that I'd lost my keys?" Mum says.

"No, Mum. I'll go and look for them in a moment."

*

After Erin leaves and Mum has been put to bed, I tidy up the kitchen and replace the filled bin liner. As it's early July, if I don't do it right away it will smell. Not to mention the fact that I once came downstairs to find Mum picking discarded chicken out of the bin. Even the memory makes my stomach churn.

The evening is pleasant and warm, but the air is full of midges. I pad down the path to the outside bin and quickly throw the filled bin liner into it.

Our garden needs tending. Mum always loved to garden, but since the Alzheimer's, she's not cared for it as much. I try to get her involved every now and then, but she's too easily distracted.

Perhaps I'll enjoy a nice, cool glass of wine when I get inside. Or maybe I'll take it into the garden and stretch out on the sun lounger. I don't drink a lot, but there's little that's more relaxing than a glass or two at home.

I frown as I step on an oddly shaped object. I didn't bother with shoes to take out the bin. It didn't seem worth it. Now my bare foot is standing on a small, round item. Too flat to be a stone. I step back, bend down, and pick it up.

It's a button from a coat or a jacket. There's nothing unusual about that, but for some reason, it seems so out of place. I know it's not from any of my clothes, and I know most of Mum's clothes. I don't think it's hers. I suppose it probably belongs to Erin, so I pop it in my jeans pocket and open the French doors into the kitchen.

"Has that shadow been hanging around again?"

I start. Mum is standing in the centre of the kitchen with her hair bedraggled and her face vacant. Her nightgown has come loose, so I can see far more of her chest than I'd like.

"Come on, Mum. I'll take you back to bed."

But before I take her up, I make sure to turn

around and lock the door. The word "shadow" pokes at a long-forgotten memory. It's there, but I can't access it, like a word on the tip of my tongue. All I know is that the word makes me shiver, and it makes me want to lock the door.

CHAPTER TWO

Through sleep-filled, bleary eyes, I somehow manage to move my finger across my phone screen to turn off the alarm. My eyelids flutter as I force myself not to choose the snooze option. I don't have time to snooze. I have too much to do.

First, I wash and dress Mum. She never was an early riser, and now that we need home help, I have to force her out of bed at 6am. Every morning, I get called every name under the sun. She's always more disorientated in the mornings. She flails her thin arms, scratches my skin with her fingernails, and hisses at me between her teeth. She finds old wounds to pick at, even in this confused state. My jaw is a favourite. I need exercise, because I'm too fat and I'll never find a man. Then there's blaming me for Dad's death. I've never amounted to anything.

I'm a disappointment.

At 6:30 I make us both breakfast. Sometimes Mum still loves her favourite breakfast, which is toast and strawberry jam. Other days, she suddenly hates it. I manage to gobble down tea and toast while watching her like a hawk to make sure she eats enough. Then at 7am Erin arrives, and I bomb upstairs to get a quick shower and get ready for work. Sometimes I even squeeze in some marking if Erin is a bit early.

It can be hard to leave the house if Mum is being difficult. I know Erin is being paid a wage to care for my mother, but I also know it's not easy, not even when she's more lucid. She's always been a difficult woman, but I suppose I found ways of dealing with it early on. I fell into a book or into my studies.

Mum never wanted me to go to university. She wanted me at home. I think she was afraid of being alone. We compromised, and I lived at home and travelled into Derby to study there. I managed to find a work placement on the outskirts of Derby, and then a position opened at the local primary school. Everything fit perfectly, and I got to stay close to her. That's how it's always been. The two of us.

Until Jamie came along. We met in the pub one Friday night at the end of term piss-up with the other teachers. You could say I was a late starter in life. I managed to get through university without any hook-ups and without many messy nights out. I'm ashamed to admit I was twenty-five before I was intimate with a man. Jamie was the first guy who was interested in me, and I grew to like him after a few weeks of him pursuing me.

He was the brother of one of the teachers at school, and worked as an electrician for a local firm. At first I wasn't interested. He was quiet, and short, and there was nothing remarkable about him. He had milky-blond hair and small blue eyes. He offered to buy me a drink and I said yes because I was drunk. Later that night we were kissing, but I went home alone after giving him my phone number.

Alisha, my colleague at the primary school and best friend, was determined that I should go out with him, but I avoided his calls for a few days until he turned up to the pub again and insisted on buying me a drink. After getting a little drunk, I finally agreed to go out with him to dinner and a movie.

Jamie never gave up. There were flowers and chocolates and bottles of wine. Mum told me that all he was interested in was a quick shag, and once I'd put out, I'd never hear from him again. But that didn't happen. He stuck around for seven years, and I finally began to love him. But Mum drove him away with her snide remarks and backhanded compliments. Every argument we ever had revolved around Mum: about the things she said to put us down, about how I wouldn't move out of her house, and when I did move out of her house, the arguments became about how we spent too much time with her. Jamie wanted to get married and have children, but there was always something holding me back. Now, I think it might have been Mum's influence. Her little comments might have planted the seeds of doubt, but I let them grow until they became tangled weeds strangling the life out of our relationship.

"If you marry him, you can't get out of it. Marriage is for life," she'd say. "Do you honestly want that lump for the rest of your life? What if there's someone better out there? Jamie couldn't find two brain cells to rub together. Is that the man you want to spend the rest of your life with?"

Somewhere buried under all her insults was a nugget of truth that wore away at me. I *didn't* want to marry Jamie. I *did* worry that there was someone else out there for me. After seven years we finally called it a day. I still blame my mother, but perhaps that isn't fair. While I rarely ever disobey her, I think I would have if Jamie had been right for me.

At least, that's what I keep telling myself.

One thing I do know is that Peter is not the guy, either.

At 7am on the dot, Erin steps into the house and waves cheerfully at us both. I'm sat next to Mum making sure she eats her cereal, with a cooling mug of tea clutched in both hands. Mum eyes Erin and frowns.

"You again," she says. "You'd best not feed me poison this time."

"Mum, this is Erin—"

"I know who this is," she snaps. "I'm not a child."

I roll my eyes for Erin's benefit.

"Good morning to you, Mrs. Howland. You're looking well today," Erin says, knowing that compliments work best with my mother.

"She almost got my hair right," Mum says.

I can't help but smile. That's about as good as it gets when it comes to compliments from Mum.

"I'd best get to school," I say. "There's ham in the fridge for sandwiches and some chocolate in the cupboard. Help yourself to whatever you fancy."

"Have a good day," Erin says. "Don't work too hard. Oh, and make sure my nephew doesn't give you any lip!"

I laugh. "Oh, he's cheeky, but sweet with it. But I'll tell him that his Aunty will be having words if he goes too far."

Eddington is a small village where everyone knows everyone, and if you work at a school you get to know all the names and faces. It's the kind of traditional place that still has a village fete at the school attended by everyone—part of the haemorrhaging English culture that everyone bemoans as it dies, but no one actually wants to revive. Erin's nephew, Noah, is in my class. He's a sweet kid, with the same blue eyes as Erin. But she's right, he can be lippy. They all can, but I don't mind. At ten years old, a little bit of cheek is expected from happy kids. It's the quiet ones I worry about the most.

I leave Mum and Erin and hop into my Fiesta, piling up the passenger seat with marking. At 7:45am I park the car, carry the pile of marking into my classroom, sit down in my chair behind the desk and breathe for the first time this morning. I fill up my lungs, close my eyes, and breathe. The place smells like whiteboard marker and glue, but I love it. This is my break from it all, and yes, it's stressful, loud and chaotic, but it's a part of my life that I control. This is *mine*.

There's work to be done. I have photocopying to do, posters to hang, notes to make, and a little extra marking to finish up, all before the kids get here. First things first: the photocopying. If I leave it too late, there'll be a queue. I pick up my lesson plans and worksheets and head down to the teacher's lounge. A cup of coffee would be good, too.

"Soph!"

I grin. "Morning, 'Lish. I see you got to the photocopier early this morning."

"Just avoiding the hoards." Alisha exaggerates an eye-roll. We've worked together for almost ten years, after both starting within six months of completing teacher training. We were a crutch for each other, both completely in it up to our ears and struggling along. "Fucking thing. I've changed the toner twice and unjammed it already this morning." She gives the ancient printer a little kick. "There's fresh coffee if you want some."

"You're a life saver. I had to peel myself out of

bed this morning."

I head over to the small kitchen area to pour a cup into my favourite mug—one with a bust of Shakespeare on the front and the caption *2B or not 2B, that is the classroom*—a present from Alisha when I first started teaching in 2B.

"How is the old battle-axe?" Alisha's posture changes when she mentions my mum. She folds her arms and narrows her eyes.

Alisha has only met Mum once, when she picked us both up from a teacher's convention in Nottingham. Unfortunately, Mum talked to Alisha like a child the whole way home, raising her voice and talking slowly, as though Alisha couldn't understand English. Alisha, whose heritage is Indian but who was born and bred in Manchester, gritted her teeth and put on an over-the-top Indian accent to make light of the situation. But I know it annoyed her—rightly so—and she's disliked Mum ever since.

I'd never gone into a lot of detail about my childhood, but I think Alisha saw who Mum truly is. Though I already knew Mum's true colours, I saw them reflected back to me from Alisha's reaction. It unsettled me.

After that incident, we almost drifted apart. It was around the same time that she became pregnant with her first child. As well as feeling incredibly awkward about how Mum had treated my best friend—and how I'd failed to stand up to Mum yet again—the sight of my best friend going through pregnancy was almost too hard to bear. It took me a long time to realise how jealous I was of her, and then I felt like the pettiest person in the world. So I shouldered the pain, and I bought presents for her newborn. I went to the hospital and I took her flowers and I held her child in my arms. I saw her happiness, and I was glad she got to experience it. I loved them both.

I try to shake the thoughts away. "Confused, frustrated, difficult. The Alzheimer's is progressing quickly. She has her good moments where she's exactly as she was, but there are times when she looks at me and I'm not sure she even knows who I am."

Alisha's expression softens. "That must be hard." She shifts her weight from one foot to the other, and an awkward silence follows. I know exactly what she's going to say next, and I automatically tense up. "Have you given it any more thought?" She raises her eyebrows, clocking me with a serious gaze.

"I have thought about it," I say. "But I can't."

It's almost imperceptible, but Alisha's lips tighten, as though she knew I was going to say that and is disappointed in me. "I'm just going to say this. I know it's not my place, but you're my best friend and I can't hold it in anymore. Why are you still caring this for woman when I *know* she's been a terrible mother to you all your life?" She holds her hands up when I'm about to interject. "It doesn't take a genius to work it out. That woman is emotionally abusive. She tried to talk you out of going to university, she picks on the way you look in front of other people, and she broke up your relationship with Jamie. God knows what she was like when you were a child. This is your opportunity to get rid of her for good and finally move on with your life. Take it. Sell her house, move her into a home, and finally live the happy life you've always deserved."

My spine straightens. "Opportunity? I'd hardly call watching my mother deteriorate into a child an opportunity."

Alisha sighs. "You're right. I'm sorry. That was a poor choice of words." She collects her papers and taps them against the top of the photocopier to get them straight. "Maybe I overstepped. I don't know. I just want to make sure that someone is on your side. I *want* to be on your side, and I want you to be happy. You know you deserve to be happy, right?"

I blink, trying to process everything that's going on: Alisha's sudden plea, Mum's difficulties at home. It's all happening so fast. A few months ago Mum had mild memory loss and lapses in concentration; now she's deteriorating faster than even the doctors expected. "I know." But I speak quietly, without confidence.

Alisha places a hand on my arm. "If you need any help, I'm right here."

I believe her, but I wonder how much help she'd be willing to offer. There's only so much anyone can do when you're in this situation. They can't clean up my mother's urine or put her to bed. They can't fill out the paperwork needed to sort out financial aid or finalise Mum's will. They can't be there 24/7, watching her to make sure she doesn't burn down the house or try to eat uncooked bacon from the refrigerator. No, they can't do any of that.

Which is Alisha's point, isn't it? That I can't cope on my own, so I should put Mum in a home. I place my paper in the photocopying machine. No. I can't do that. Mum would give up in a place like that. I wouldn't be able to afford the best, and I'd be leaving my mother at the mercy of people who probably don't give a shit about their patients. There are horror stories in the press all the time, detailing how care assistants abuse their patients. I can't let that happen to Mum, no matter what has happened to us, no matter how hard the next few years will be.

*

The classroom is one of the few places I can clear my mind of all the things I need to do to help Mum. This is all about the children, and giving them a good start in life. But I'm the first to admit that my head is all over the place today. I even mess up teaching a simple grammar lesson to the children, prompting Isaac—who is very advanced for his age—to question me. My face grows red, and all the children make *oooh* and *ahhh* noises when I realise my mistake. Erin's nephew calls out, "Miss, Miss, you got it wrong, Miss!", delighted that a grown-up can make a mistake.

Lunch time is a sandwich at my desk followed by playground duty. I quickly check my phone for messages. Erin has texted: *Mum doing well today. Ate all her lunch and is watching* Loose Women *on TV! See you later. Xoxo.* I couldn't ask for a better nurse. She truly is a godsend.

I also have a text from Peter: *Enjoyed our coffee (Coke for me!). Hope your mum is ok. Shall we rearrange?* There's also a missed call from him. He's put a lot of effort in so far, although it verges on creepy. Maybe I should give him another chance. I mull it over in my mind, thinking about his attitude toward books. That could be a deal-breaker. Maybe it's best to leave it. He seems pretty keen, though, which could result in an awkward telephone call. I cringe at the thought.

The bell goes for playtime to end, and the children start filtering back into the school. There's one girl lagging behind the others, Chloe, a sweet but quiet girl who tends to play on her own during the break. My heart breaks when the others tease or ostracise her. She's not quite as developed as the rest of the class. She often struggles with her reading. I watch her as she makes her way into the school. There's something else about Chloe... something odd.

"Come on, Jessie," Chloe says, holding her arm out as though she's dragging someone behind her, except that there's no one behind her. She gives her wrist a little shake as though yanking them forward. "You're too slow! I have to get to class."

"Hi, Chloe. Are you ready for this afternoon's class?" I ask, trying to get her attention away from her imaginary friend. I read a little child psychology during my training as a teacher, so I know it's normal to have an imaginary friend, but it's odd for her to be ten and still have one, *and* for her to play with her imaginary friend at school rather than make actual friends.

"Yes," she whispers. Her small head of blonde hair passes me, and she walks into the entrance of the school and down the hall. I frown, worrying again about the quiet children in my class, the ones who are forgotten and ignored. It's my duty to look out for them. That's how it works. Those of us who live through it grow up and give back because we know how hard it was.

My mind is still on Chloe as I travel home from work with a daunting stack of homework to mark. Most teachers I know hate how much homework young children are forced to endure, and how many standardised tests they're made to sit to. We hate the stats and the OFSTED side of teaching. We want to give the children the best education we can, but the restrictions force us into becoming clones of each other, delivering clone messages to mini-clones.

I pause at my front door, expecting to hear shouting or glass breaking, but the house is quiet.

When I step into the hall and shed my coat, the place is oddly serene.

"Sophie, is that you?" Erin calls out.

"Yes. Is everything all right? It seems very…" When I walk into the living room, Mum is sat on the sofa with a cup of tea. Her face is slack. No matter how often I see her like that, I'll never get used to it. It's like seeing only the shell of a person.

"We're all fine," Erin says. "You look shattered. Was Noah a nuisance?"

I laugh, but it sounds hollow. "He was an angel."

"Yeah, yeah. Cuppa?"

"I'd love one."

I follow Erin into the kitchen, which is our after-work ritual. I could see us as friends even after… after what? After Mum dies? That's the only way this ends.

"I boiled the kettle a moment ago," Erin says. "I knew you'd be home soon."

"You're an angel too, just like your nephew!"

She laughs, and her face lights up. Her eyes twinkle. I'm jealous then, for a moment. She gets to go home and relax with her boyfriend. She can shake off the day and forget all about my mother. I have to think about her all day, and it's wearing me out.

"Oh, I almost forgot." I lift my bag onto the breakfast bar and rummage through it. "I found this in the garden last night, by the back door. I think it must be yours, because it's not mine or

Mum's." I pass her the button.

Erin lifts it and frowns at it. "You must have the wrong person. It's not mine. I don't have anything in that shade, and I always wear my nurse's uniform here, anyway."

She passes it back to me and starts pouring the hot water over tea bags.

I turn the smooth, round button over between my fingers. If it isn't mine, Mum's or Erin's, that means someone else has been in our garden.

CHAPTER THREE

Before I go to sleep, I tell myself that there are a dozen possible explanations as to how someone else's button ended up in our garden. It could have been someone from the gas or electric supplier. *But why would he go to the back door?* It could have been in the neighbour's rubbish and blown onto our property. *There hasn't been any strong wind for weeks.* Or an animal could have been playing with it and left it in the garden. Maybe it was the tabby cat from across the road, or a fox, or even a bird. Yes, that must be it. An animal dropped it in the back garden. I drift into slumber dreaming about packs of foxes tearing our rubbish bags apart and dropping buttons everywhere.

"Get up. I said, get up. There was someone in my room."

"What?"

Cold fingers wrap around my wrist, jerking me

up before I can fully open my eyes. Fingernails dig into my skin.

"There was someone in my room." Mum's voice is a raspy whisper. In the gloom, her dark eyes lower towards my face, unsettling me to my core.

"You're hurting my arm. Mum, let me go." When she releases me, I pull back the duvet and swing my legs down to the floor. My heart is beating fast.

"There was someone in my room, but they're gone now," she says again.

"All right, come on, let's check." My arm is shaking as I gently place it behind her thin shoulders. My eyes flick around the room, scanning for some kind of weapon. What can I do if there's a burglar in the house? I'm not exactly strong or fast. I grab my mobile phone from under my pillow and move Mum out of my bedroom. She's probably confused. There's no one here.

I turn on the lights in Mum's room, then check the wardrobe and under the bed with sweat forming on my back. I've watched enough detective shows on TV to know that serial killers always hide under the bed.

"There's no one here, Mum," I say, beginning to relax.

"Check the house," she insists.

We take the stairs together, two scrawny women in their nightgowns. My heart still patters beneath my skin, pumping blood up to my ears. Mum grips the banister so hard her knuckles are white. We don't speak.

The house is quiet. That means there's little likelihood that someone is actually in the house. If a burglar had broken in, they'd be making noise trying to steal our TV or computer. I hurry through every room, turning on all the lights and checking every corner. I grip my phone, ready to call 999 at even the slightest sound. There's nothing. I check the doors and windows. Everything is locked.

"It's okay, Mum. There's no one here. Let's go back to bed." I check the time on my phone. It's 4am. I groan.

"There was someone in my room," she says again.

"They've gone now, Mum. Everything is safe," I say.

Her eyes are narrowed, lethal. The hairs on the back of my arms stand on end. Her lips purse together.

"You're a disappointment," she says in a hiss.

I can't help it; tears prick at the back of my eyes. I take a moment to breathe, composing myself, then I direct her back to bed.

*

At 6am, I press snooze. At 6:05, I hear the sound of my mother's feet moving around the house and I'm up in an instant. I hurry downstairs to find her standing triumphantly in the middle of the kitchen, waving her keys in the air.

"I found them!" she says. "They were dropped behind the kitchen bin."

"That's great," I reply, trying to force some cheer into my voice. There's only so much cheer to be found after broken sleep. "Let's get you dressed. Aren't you tired? We were up half the night."

"No, we weren't," she says. "What are you talking about?"

"You thought someone was in your room, remember?" In my exhausted state, I forget to pander to her. I snap at her instead, and she appears taken aback by my sharp tongue.

"You think I'm stupid." She slams the keys down on the counter and squares her shoulders. "Well, I'm not stupid. You're the idiot. You always have been."

"Yes, yes, I know. Come on. We need to get ready before Erin arrives."

"Who's Erin?"

My shoulders sag. I'm not sure I can do this today. It's hard enough when I've had a restful night. Luckily, Mum is distracted by moving up the stairs. She forgets all about Erin and the keys and whatever else has been on her mind. I manage to get her into her room.

"I can do it," Mum says, snatching her arm away from me.

"Fine." I pass her the clothes and walk out.

Space. That's what I need. A few moments to compose myself, to rid my mind of its crippling stresses. Two minutes alone. My bedroom is filled with comforting silence until my mobile phone begins to buzz. I retrieve it from underneath the pillow to find another missed call from Peter. That makes over half a dozen missed calls from him over the last few days, and a fair few unanswered text messages. I'm not a dating expert, but so many attempts to contact me are making me uncomfortable. I'm going to have to call him back and put a stop to this. You'd think he would have got the message already, but clearly not, and I don't want to lead him on.

My bedroom door opens and Mum stands in the doorway in a smart dress, a pair of heeled court shoes and a cashmere cardigan. There's a neat slick of lipstick on her lips and some powder on her cheeks. "What are you doing in here? Where's my breakfast?"

It takes me a minute to know what to say. There are moments through watching this awful disease disassemble my mother that she is so like the woman I used to know that it knocks all the wind out of me and I'm at an absolute loss for words. All I can do is follow her down to the kitchen and pour cereal into bowls.

"Yoo-hoo, anybody home?" Erin breezes into the house and relieves the tension in the air. "Oh, wow, Mrs. Howland, you're looking *fantastic* today. I love that outfit. Can I borrow it?"

"Not likely," Mum says. "You'll stretch it out."

Erin bites her lip to stop herself from laughing. I suppose mean old people are pretty hilarious.

Unless they're your parent, that is.

"Time for a cuppa?" Erin asks.

I glance at my phone. "I'd better shower and get ready for work."

"Are you all right this morning? You don't seem yourself."

"Mum woke up in the night and thought someone was in her room." Saying it out loud brings the fear back, making me almost spill milk as I pass Mum her cereal bowl. "There was no one there, of course. But it meant I didn't get much sleep."

"I bet." Erin chews on her bottom lip and tilts her head to one side sympathetically. "She's getting to be a bit of a handful, isn't she? How are you coping with it all?"

"I have good days and bad days." Mostly bad. And apparently I look awful, because everyone keeps telling me that. "I should probably get ready." I flash her a smile and scurry out of the room, glad to be away from them both.

*

First I tell myself I'll call Peter on the way to work. Then I say I'll do it during the first break. Before I know it, lunch time is almost here and I still haven't called him. If he hadn't called me so many times, I'd feel a lot better about it. It's not particularly *normal* to call someone over and over like that. And then there's the text messages, which started off friendly and ended up needy: *Hi Sophie, just checking in about our second date. Get back to me!* And then the latest one: *Ok, I just want to know you're all right. Get in touch. Pleaaase xx.* We hardly know each other. We had five minutes of conversation. Why does he care so much about my welfare?

There's a big red flag waving over Peter's head right now, and I'm not sure what to do. If there's a way to make this situation worse, there's a good chance I'll find it. That's the way the world works, right?

"Miss! Miss!"

The pink palm waving in front of my face alerts me to the fact that I've been staring at my phone for several minutes.

"Can we go to lunch now? The bell rang."

"It did?"

The entire class choruses, "Duh!"

I wave my hand at them. "Go on, then. Get gone!"

As the children filter out of the room, my phone begins to vibrate. The sound is amplified by the hard surface of my desk, and every one of my muscles clench. I snatch the phone up and stare at the screen. When I see that it's Erin calling, I'm at first relieved, and then nervous. I answer.

"Is everything okay?"

"I'm so sorry, Sophie," she says. "But I think you need to come home. Your mum won't settle today."

I can hear that Erin is on the brink of tears. "Has she hit you?"

"No... well... she's been very difficult and won't eat at all. She tried to leave the house, and I had to stop her. She tried to steal my car keys. She kept muttering about the house not feeling safe. She's seems frightened, but I don't know why."

"All right. I'm going to come home early. I won't be long."

I hang up the phone and hurry out to the playground where I know Alisha is on duty. When she sees me, she frowns.

"Are you okay?"

"I'm fine, but I have to go home. The nurse is having trouble with Mum, and I need to be there. Can my class go in with yours after the break?"

"Of course," she says. "What are you going to do about Moira, though?"

"Thank you. I'll have to square it with her on my way home."

Alisha's concerned gaze follows me as I hurry back into the school. Moira—our pocket-sized monster of a head teacher—won't be happy, but there's nothing I can do. Sometimes, family takes priority over work and that's all there is to it.

I knock on the door to the head teacher's office. Then I wait. Her secretary is on her lunch break, so I have to wait for Moira herself.

"Come in."

I enter the room and am face to face with Moira's ice-blue eyes, always shocking beneath her sharp cut of black hair. She sits stiffly, with her hands placed on the desk in front of her. There's no trace of a smile, and I immediately feel as though I'm a child again.

Despite Moira's reputation as a battle-axe with the school board, and her zero tolerance for staff members who don't pull their weight, Moira MacIntosh is a favourite with the children. They call her Mac, and she tells irreverent jokes to the kids in assembly, throwing in pop culture references and commanding their attention like no one else can in the entire school.

"I'm so sorry. I have to go home this afternoon. It's my mum."

"Is everything all right?" she asks.

"Yes... well, no... she's deteriorating fast. The nurse is having problems with her. I'm so sorry. This won't be a habit, I promise. Alisha has room for my children in her class."

She nods her head once. "Okay. That should be fine this once." There's the smallest flash of a smile before her gaze is redirected to the work on her desk.

I back out of the room feeling a little put out by such a curt dismissal. My neck warms with embarrassment. I went in expecting reassurance and was given none. It could be my imagination, but did she chastise me with her little smile and laconic words? *That should be fine* this once. I certainly have that hot sensation of being chastised. My palms are sweaty as I walk through the corridors feeling as though everyone is turning to stare at me. At least, it was certainly a reminder that this can't happen again. This is the first time I've ever gone home early from work.

As I hurry to the carpark, I try to put those thoughts behind me. Getting home is my concern right now. I'm running on adrenaline and caffeine as I drive home. I'm floating along on fumes, getting ready to self-destruct. At least I manage to get home without hurting myself or anyone else.

My heels scrape along the path as I rush to the door. It's locked, so I have to fumble with my keys and then push through into the hall. I turn and lock the door again. Erin must have locked it for a reason. Probably to stop my mother rushing out.

"Erin? Mum?"

The sound of raised voices comes from the living room. *Something... something... you're not welcome here. Something... out of my house.* Then there's a sob.

When I enter, I find Erin cowering behind the sofa cushion with Mum holding the heavy candlestick we use for church candles above her head. I approach slowly, shocked at the scene before me.

"Mum, put the candlestick down."

She turns to me, and her mouth falls open. "This woman is in my house, and she won't let me drive. I want to go for a drive."

"If you give me the candlestick, we can go for a drive."

Her eyes flash with anger for a moment and I take a step back, anxious about what she'll do. Then her arms lower and she blinks. "I'm not sure I want to go for a drive after all. I think I want to go to bed."

"That's okay, Mum. Let's put you to bed."

"I… I think I need to go—"

"I'm so sorry, Erin. You get off. I can cope here."

"Are you sure?" She wipes her wet cheeks and grasps for her handbag on the coffee table.

"Of course."

The front door slams before we're even halfway up the stairs. It's not like I'm not used to being alone with my mother—that's how it's been for pretty much all of my life—but now it feels very lonely.

"Do you remember Dad?" The question pops out before I can retrieve it. I tense up as we shuffle through the bedroom door and Mum sits on the edge of the bed. Even before the Alzheimer's, Mum hated talking about my father. I don't remember much about him, only that he committed suicide when I was very young. Mum was furious about him leaving her with a child to take care of. She barely spoke about him ever again.

"Soft," she says. "Soft eyes. Soft will." She shakes her head. "I never told you."

"Told me what?" I turn to face her so I can see the expression on her face. It's such an odd thing to say. Ominous, even, suggesting there are secrets in our past.

"What are you talking about?" she asks.

I sigh. Whatever secrets my mother has will probably stay that way. I'm not sure she'll ever be coherent enough to tell me. I peel off her cardigan and help her onto the bed.

"Mum, what's..." I examine her arms. There are purple marks all over her skin. Bad ones. Her arms are more purple than the usual sallow pink of her skin. "What happened to you?"

"I already told you," she says. "It was the shadow."

CHAPTER FOUR

In my late twenties and early thirties, I watched my friends have children. I don't have many friends, at least not anymore, but there were people I'd kept in touch with after uni, as well as my colleagues at the school. I'd ask them how they did it, how they survived on no sleep when their little ones went through troubled nights. How did they get up for work the next day and act like a human being? Most people admitted it was hard and that they did it because they had no other choice. Others gave me soppy answers, that they ran on "love and cuddles", which—broody as I was back then—brought up a little of my lunch.

Alisha put it best. When her little boy, Dan, was two years old, he had difficulty sleeping through the night. She told me one day when she was particularly exhausted that there is no magic way of dealing without sleep. Our bodies need it. Sure, we can run on fumes, caffeine, and sheer force of will for a while, but it changes us. We become snappy and argumentative to those we love. But it makes you prioritise everything in life. It gets rid of the bullshit.

I'm not there yet. I'm still able to sleep. I have to get up in the night to reassure Mum again that there's no one in her room, checking every nook and cranny so she can relax, but I still manage a good few hours before the alarm goes off. I'm tired; my limbs feel heavier than usual, and it takes me a while to come round, but I have enough energy to face the day. What worries me is the niggle in the back of my mind. I can't run on "love and cuddles". Caring for a person suffering with this terrible disease is not full of joy and kisses. Where am I going to find that last bit of energy? How am I going to survive when it all gets to be too much?

Part of me didn't expect Erin to come back. I braced myself for a new nurse to knock on the door this morning. But Erin enters the house with a little wave to me and a hesitant smile to Mum.

I hand her a cup of tea. "About yesterday —"

"It's my fault," she says. "I've been trained to handle patients when they're being difficult. It all happened so suddenly that I got overwhelmed."

"Erin." I sigh, wrapping my hand around my mug for warmth. "Mum is more than difficult; I know that. And I know that not all of it is from the Alzheimer's. Some of her nastiness is just her. I'm so sorry about yesterday. I wish there was more I could do."

"It's fine," she says. I can see the effort she's putting into trying to sound breezy. I can see how her smile is forced. I wouldn't want her job either.

"I'm going to take her back to the doctor soon. Maybe there's something he can prescribe to make her calmer."

"Oh, no," Erin replies. "I wouldn't want her to suffer because of me. She's still herself a lot of the time. I'd hate to take that away from her."

I think of Mum as herself. I think of her sharp eyes and sharper tongue. Perhaps there's a part of me that would enjoy taking that away, but I shake the thought away. It's a nasty, bitter thought that leaves a sour taste in my mouth.

"And don't worry about the bruises. They seem bad, but I checked, and her movement is fine. She has quite delicate skin, as older people tend to have. I know you had to restrain her, so don't worry about it." I stop talking and watch as Erin's expression changes to utter shock. Her eyes widen and she tugs on an earring.

"What bruises? I don't know what you mean."

"I think you must have bruised her arms when you stopped her getting out of the house. Like I said, it's fine. I know you'd never intentionally hurt Mum, and you had to stop her leaving or she might have run out into the road or worse."

"But I didn't restrain her." Erin's voice is high-pitched and agitated. There's a red flush working its way up her neck. "I would never hurt her. She hurt me by hitting me on my arm, but I didn't even mention it because—"

"I'm sorry. I didn't mean to accuse you of anything. I noticed a few bruises when I put her to bed yesterday, and I presumed... I'm sure it happened some other way. Did you see her bang herself? Walk into any furniture?"

"No," she says, rubbing a hand across her neck. "I didn't see anything like that, and I was watching her the entire time. I don't know how she could have hurt herself like that. I'll take a look at them today, if you like."

"Thanks. That would be great."

The silence that follows is tense and awkward. Erin sips her tea without meeting my gaze. I check my phone and realise I'm going to be late for work if I don't hurry, so I slip up the stairs. As I shimmy out of my dressing gown and turn on the shower, I try to ignore the creeping sense of unease that washes over me. Firstly, I initiated a change in our relationship by accusing Erin of hurting Mum. I hadn't meant it to be an accusation. I was so sure that she'd had to restrain Mum that I made a presumption and put my foot in it. Secondly, if it wasn't Erin, and Mum didn't bang into any furniture during the day, how did she get the bruises?

*

While I usually like to get my kids to interact in the

classroom, there are times when it's nice to let them read quietly while I finish marking. Today I decide that the afternoon lesson can be half reading their books quietly to themselves, and the other half reading passages aloud to the class with a little discussion afterwards. I know that every teacher tries to get the shy kids out of their shell a little, and pretty much every teacher fails to do so, but I have a few children that I'd like to read aloud today. It's tough for them, I know, but I worry about how they'll interact with the world when they're older. I remember the first time I had to speak aloud in a professional capacity and how terrified I was. I don't want them to feel that way.

"Okay, I need some volunteers. Who's going to read the first paragraph? How about you, Chloe?"

I ignore the other hands that go up. I know Ben will read it in a funny voice and probably insert a few fart noises. Alice will sit up straight and put on her poshest voice, showing off for the rest of the class. It's not Alice and Ben that I worry about. It's Chloe. The girl the other ones ignore. The girl who stares out of the window with a woeful expression.

The girl who stares at me with a look of abject terror on her face. "Which bit, Miss?" She moves around in her seat and picks up the book, pretending to search for the paragraph in question.

"At the top of the page, Chloe. It starts with 'The penguins…'."

She stares intently at the page. Her fingers pull the book apart, stretching the spine. She finally lifts her head and says, "Can Jessie read it?"

The class breaks out into giggles.

"That's enough," I say in my sternest voice. "Would it help if Jessie read the paragraph?"

Chloe nods her head up and down. My heart sinks. She's so behind the others in literacy and numeracy that I'm not sure how I'm going to help her.

"Then you can read it as Jessie if you like." I use my kind but serious voice to try to stop any giggling or nonsense from the rest of the class. "Off you go."

"The…. Pen… Gins," she begins.

Unfortunately, as she speaks as her imaginary friend Jessie, she uses an odd, nasal voice that makes most of the class spasm with barely controlled silent laughter. I give Ben an icy stare as he begins to open his mouth to speak. I shush others who can't keep their laughter quiet.

"That's okay, Chloe. You're doing well." I nod at her, encouraging her to go on when she trips over words. Finally, she comes to the end of the paragraph. "Well done, Chloe. That was great. Okay, who's next? How about you, Alice?" A safe bet. Alice is far too in need of approval from me to make fun of Chloe's reading. She picks up where Chloe left off, pronouncing each word with aplomb.

I hardly hear her. I'm watching Chloe. She doesn't even appear to be aware of the rest of the class. She's scribbling notes on scrap paper and showing them to an invisible person sat next to her. Then she smiles.

"...and that is why penguins are the only bird..."

The bell goes, snapping me out of my reverie. "Okay, guys, off to break time you go. No running in the corridor." I wait in my seat as the children rush out of the room, finally free to laugh as loud as they want. They're fuelled by the held-in excitement. Friends turn to each other and whisper about Chloe. Others imitate her odd voice. I wait until Chloe is passing my desk and then I ask her to stop for a moment.

"How are you, Chloe? You're a little withdrawn from the class today."

"I'm okay," she says.

"You read well today. I'd like you to keep practicing your reading, okay?"

She nods.

If there's any trace of embarrassment or sadness from today's class, I can't see it. She's impassive but clearly uncomfortable talking to me. She'd rather be hidden away with Jessie in some corner of the playground.

"What about your parents? Are they okay?" I ask.

"They're fine." She stares down at her hands.

"Have fun at break today. Are you going to play with the others?"

She shakes her head. "Just Jessie."

I catch movement in the corner of my eye.

Alisha stands in the doorway waving.

"Okay, well, see you in class after break," I say, dismissing Chloe.

Alisha strides into the classroom and perches on one of the front desks. She watches Chloe leave the room, shutting the door behind her like I ask the children to do if they're last out of the classroom. I like a few moments of peace.

"That kid gives me the creeps." She unwraps a chocolate bar and tucks in.

"I'm trying to get her to interact with the other kids, but nothing I do works. In fact, I end up making it worse. Now they're all teasing her." I sigh and run my fingers through my hair.

"The parents have hired a child psychologist," Alisha says. "She seems disturbed, if you ask me."

"Well, at least the psychologist might be able to do something. They'll be more help than I am, anyway."

"Hey, you want to go for a coffee after work? I'll get you a mocha and a bun." Alisha waggles her eyebrows at me, trying to entice me out.

"I can't. I need to be at home after Mum's bad episode yesterday."

"You need some time away from her *and* work," Alisha says. "You look like you're about to burn out."

"I'll be okay," I reply, wondering whether that's a lie.

"Be careful, Soph. You can't fix everyone who makes you feel sorry for them."

*

I'm playing Alisha's words over and over in my mind as I make my way home from work. Is that what I'm trying to do? Fix everyone around me? Is that why I worry about Chloe, even though she isn't my child? My mind is not on the road, and I cut off a driver when I pull out of a junction. There's a loud beeping of the horn from behind me, so I put my foot down and hurry along.

With everything that's going on, it's only natural for my imagination to run wild. Perhaps I'm unintentionally seeking out problems where I don't need to. Chloe has parents and a family. I should leave her in their safekeeping.

Her face is on my mind as I pull onto my street and search for a parking space. Only a few houses have driveways. The streets are cramped with cars.

Then it comes to me.

Chloe reminds me of myself when I was a child.

School was difficult for me. I didn't have many friends; I was withdrawn. I even had an imaginary friend when I was little. What I want is to go back and help the younger version of me.

The thought is unsettling, but it's true. I put it to the back of my mind as I park the car, unclip my seatbelt, and make my way into the house. There haven't been any calls from Erin, so I assume everything has gone smoothly today. Still, my body is strung tight as I open the door and call out hello.

I'm half expecting Erin and Mum to be going at it hammer and tongs, each trying to strangle the other, with their eyes wide and bloodshot. But all is quiet. Mum is on the sofa, zonked out in front of one of her soaps. Erin is wiping down the dining table with a cloth.

"She spilled her tea," Erin says.

I can't help but notice that she's not meeting my eyes, and she's wiping down the table rather vigorously. "Can I make you a cuppa?"

"Not today. I've got to get home. Josh is cooking dinner tonight."

"Sounds lovely."

Erin moves across the kitchen and squeezes out the cloth in the sink.

"I'm sorry about this morning," I say. "I got the wrong end of the stick. Completely."

"Don't worry about it." She puts the cloth back on the draining board and dries her hands with a towel. "Looks like your phone is ringing." She gestures to where I left it on the kitchen side. "I'd best be off. I'll see you in the morning."

There's not much more I can say, so I let her leave, hoping that she'll forgive me after sleeping on it. Peter's name is on my screen again. I take a deep breath. It's time to put a stop to all this. I try to shake out the nerves, and then answer the phone.

"Hello," I say.

"Sophie!" He sounds so excited to hear my voice that my heart almost skips a beat. "I was so worried."

"I'm sorry I haven't got back to you, Peter. It's just... well, I've been busy with my mum."

"That's okay," he says without hesitation.

"Look, I know you were hoping to meet again, but I'm really... sorry... I... umm. The thing is, I have too much going on right now. I'm pretty much caring for Mum full-time and—"

"I don't mind," he interrupts. "I live with my mum too. I think it's great that you take care of her."

"Right. And that's nice of you, but I can't fit *anything* else into my life right now."

"What are you saying, Sophie?" I might be being oversensitive, but it sounds as if his voice has taken on an icy edge. He's annoyed.

"I'm saying that there won't be a second date. It's nothing to do with you. You're very... nice. I can't... I can't date right now."

When he next speaks, it's as though he's talking through gritted teeth. "Then why did you complete the dating profile in the first place?"

I'm taken aback. I didn't expect this level of hostility. I knew he was a bit odd, and the phone calls were quite intense, but now I'm actually worried. "It was nice meeting you, Peter." My voice betrays my nerves with a slight tremor. It's physically uncomfortable for me to deal with confrontation. "I have to go now." And in a quiet voice, I add, "Please don't call me again."

I hang up, hurry through to the living room to

check Mum is still asleep, then I boot up my laptop and sit at the dining table. My heart is still beating quickly as I delete my profile from the dating website. Then I lean back in my chair and try to process what just happened. Maybe I'm overreacting. He didn't threaten me. There was nothing about *what* he said; it was *how* he said it that disturbed me.

My bones ache when I stand up to make a cup of tea. The shrill sound of the house phone startles me, and a jolt of anxious energy shoots up my spine. I place a hand on my chest to calm myself. It's probably telemarketing.

"Hello?"

Nothing.

I scratch the back of my arm. Gooseflesh spreads over my skin.

"Who's there?"

Still nothing.

"Peter?"

The caller hangs up.

CHAPTER FIVE

I place the phone back down on its base and step away. There are so many questions in my mind, but the one that stands out the most is: was that Peter? And if it was Peter, how did he get my home phone number?

"Who was that?" Mum's face is slack and puffy from her slumber. She rubs sleep away from the corner of one eye and frowns at me.

"I don't know," I say. "They hung up."

"Probably one of those people selling PPI insurance or whatever it is," she says.

It's odd to see her so lucid after a nap. She's usually confused. But this disease is so variable. She has good moments, bad moments, good days, bad days... I can't keep up.

"I don't think so," I say. "It was... I don't know."

Her eyes narrow. "What's the matter with you?

You're all pale." She takes a step towards me, and I try not to cower as her eyes scour my face, inspecting me for clues. She loves to guess when something is wrong, because she loves to be right. "You know who called." The corners of her mouth twitch up, half smiling.

It's amazing how one hard glare from my mother turns me into a ten-year-old girl who squirms as she forces the truth out of me. *Who threw stones at the car, Sophie? Tell me. It was the neighbour's kid, wasn't it? You're covering for him.* I cringe away from her, expecting those strong fingers to wrap around my arm and drag me through the house, then storm next door and bang on the door. I can feel her fingernails digging into me. I close my eyes and swallow, forcing the memory away.

"I don't know for sure," I say when I'm composed.

"Well, whoever it is, they've given you the heebie-jeebies. Come on, then. Spit it out. Who is calling our house and hanging up, and why are you scared?"

"Peter," I blurt out. "The man I met from the dating website. I think it's him, and I don't know how he got our home number. I only gave him my mobile number. He's been calling me a lot, but I thought he was a bit over-keen but harmless. Then, when I told him nothing was going to happen, he sounded quite… angry."

She sucks in a long breath and straightens her

back. Her fists clench at her sides, and I take a step back. "You *stupid* girl! I told you not to meet anyone from the internet, didn't I? I warned you this would happen. But, no, you never listen to your mother." I go cold all over as I watch her spit the words. As always, her body is completely still as her head shakes and nods with anger. Her eyes are wide now, and the sagging skin of her cheeks wobbles as she becomes more and more agitated. "You've been nothing but a little idiot all these years. Going against everything I say and *failing* at everything—"

"That's not... I haven't failed... I'm a—"

"Did I say you could speak?"

There's a moment of complete silence where I shut my mouth and wait.

Then she continues, more slowly, more deliberately. "You're nothing but a magnet for morons. What was that dumpy fool called? Jimmy?"

"Jamie."

"Of all the men you could choose, you went with that fat little man. I told you from the beginning that he was a loser, didn't I? But you let him trample all over you like the good little doormat you are." She laughs. "Of course, with that chin, you can't hope for much more than an egg-smelling fatty like *Jamie*." She imitates my voice as she says his name.

I find myself staring at my feet, like I have my entire life. Tears burn at the backs of my eyes. In the past, I've broken down completely and begged her to stop. But I know now that these outbursts are inevitable. Whenever she's stressed about anything, she takes it out on me. If I can just take it, if I can let her get all this vitriol out of her system, it'll stop, and I won't have to worry about it for a little while.

"Get a haircut and stop dressing like an eighty-year-old librarian and you might actually find a fella." She snorts. "Didn't I tell you how, years ago? Didn't I show you? I could have any man in the village if I wanted." This was perhaps true ten years ago, when Mum was still an attractive forty-five-year-old woman. Also, she's already *had* nearly every man in the village. Her affairs are the worst-kept secret in Eddington. "How did I raise you? How did you end up this frumpy prude who needs the *internet* for a date and only attracts perverts and idiots? What did I do as a mother to deserve a daughter like you?"

The last sentence hangs in the air. It's nothing I've not heard before, but the vitriol always surprises me. I shut my eyes and a memory floats into my mind.

It's afternoon in winter, and the low setting sun floods the kitchen. I'm young, only six or seven years old, waiting for my dinner. Mum is banging pots and pans, shouting at the gas stove, which won't work. The room is freezing cold, and I'm wearing a thick jumper. Mum swears, and I stare down at my fingers, trying to block out the bad words. Then she spins around and stares at me. Her eyes are cold. She speaks in a cold voice. "It was never supposed to be you. You're not the daughter I deserve."

I open my eyes, but she's gone.

"Mum?"

There's the sound of keys jangling.

"Mum!"

I rush through the living room to see the door yanked open. "Mum, no!"

Her back disappears into the street. I hurry, calling after her, but she's quick. Narrow-shouldered, petite, and swift on her feet as she dashes out into the street. I watch in horror as the car comes towards her. She stops in the middle of the road and turns towards the car. There's a screech of brakes. I stop. Then I start again, running towards her. Her hands are out in front of her face.

"Mum? Are you all right?"

There's the slam of a car door. "She ran out right in front of me!"

I put my arm around Mum's shoulders. She's crying, wetting my blouse. "I know. I'm sorry." Mum feels frail beneath my touch. Her shoulders are bony and rigid. Old bones.

"What was she thinking?" the driver says. I get a good look at him now. He's young, with a stubbled jaw and mousy hair.

"I'm really sorry. She has dementia."

He falters. "Oh, I…"

That's right. There's nothing to say. I open my

mouth to respond, but I find nothing to say, either. I guide my mother back into the house.

"I may not be the daughter you wanted," I whisper to her. "But I'm the only person you have to care for you now."

I don't know if she hears me.

*

Night comes quickly. After the incident in the street, I make us a sausage casserole. Mum is silent throughout the entire meal. Afterwards, she looks at me and smiles, but it seems as though she's remembering someone else. Someone from her past. Then her eyes regain focus and she frowns, her hand held up towards my face as though she's going to stroke my cheek.

I take her up to bed and helped her into her nightie.

"You have to check the wardrobe for the shadow," she says.

Dutifully, I open the wardrobe doors and shift the clothes to the side so that I can check every corner.

"Mum, what is this 'shadow'? You keep mentioning it, but you won't explain what it is. Why does it seem familiar to me?"

Her mouth gapes open and then snaps shut. She shakes her head. Her eyes are so piercing that I know she's found a moment of lucidity. "I don't know what you mean. There is no shadow. It doesn't exist."

I sigh. "Good night, Mum."

"Yes," she replies.

She rolls onto her side and places her head on the pillow. I switch off the light and head downstairs to pour a large glass of wine.

From now on, I know I'll need to keep the house and car keys away from her. That's one more thing I'll need to think about every moment of the day.

I gulp down a little wine, replaying the moment the car was hurtling towards my mum. My heart beats faster and a sense of dread works its way up my body. But it isn't the fear of losing her that causes it. It's the thought I had when I saw that car coming towards her. It was only fleeting. Yes, only a split second. But it was there, and it was too loud to ignore. I can't pretend it never happened, even though I'd like to.

I thought, for one brief, tiny instant, that if the car kept going, if it hit my mum—if that car had mowed down my mother right in front of me, everything would end. She would be gone. She would no longer be suffering with this disease, with the pieces of her mind disappearing bit by bit.

And I would be free.

CHAPTER SIX

In my dream there's a mirror without a reflection. I press my hand to the mirror. It's cold, rigid. A small crack forms from the place my fingertip touches the glass. Gradually, the crack spreads across the surface as I watch in utter fascination, following the lines with my eyes as they form narrow veins. Those lines expand until the glass begins to shatter. I step away, finally pulled out of my trance, saving my hand from a multitude of cuts. I'm out of harm's reach, but I experience pain anyway. It comes from my stomach and radiates out, crushing me from the inside. That's when I realise I'm hollowed out. I'm broken up. I'm as shattered as the mirror with no reflection.

When the pain ends, the sensation that someone is watching me sweeps over my skin, as light and ticklish as the bristles of a paintbrush. I shudder from its touch, dragging my nails over my flesh.

There's darkness behind me. I sense a presence, and that presence is familiar, but I don't know why. I start to turn. Slowly. Gradually. I need to know who is behind me. The desire is instinctual. Primitive. It's as vital as breathing. The need claws at my intestines, demanding to know this presence. But this is where the dream ends, with my body half-twisted, my chest rising and falling in anticipation, and the whisper of darkness reaching out to me but not quite finding me. This is where I wake.

I open my eyes. My skin is slicked with sweat. It's slippery and cold when I rub the dreams from my eyes. The alarm blares and I lash out, tangling my hands in the bedsheets. It's 6am and my day has begun.

I find my phone and switch off the alarm. Then I swing my legs out of the bed and heave my weight up. Despite eating less and less each day, I feel heavier. It's not body fat that's weighing me down, it's stress. It's the knowledge that I'll spend another day worrying. The pressure of caring for my failing mother is dragging me down, and I can't deny it any longer.

At least the soft cotton of my dressing gown is comforting. I walk across my room and open a window. There's a bitter scent in the air. Perhaps it's my body odour from the nightmare. Perhaps it's the basket of laundry overflowing from neglect. The morning breeze is fresh and pleasant on my skin. I could linger here for another minute, maybe three or five, but I can't. I need to get ready.

My feet drag across the carpet on my way out of the room. When did my steps slow to a crawl? I used to be swift. On school trips, my pupils complained that they couldn't keep up, but I'd tell them not to dawdle because there was so much I wanted to show them. So much art, so much literature, so much technology.

The door shuts behind me with a firm *clunk*. The handle of Mum's door is cold, and it triggers an image from my dream, of my fingertips pressing the glass of the mirror. I shake the image away and open the door.

The smell hits me first. It fills the room. Vomit. Then I hear her. I hear the strangled sound coming from her throat, like a growl bubbling through soup. Her skin is waxy and pale. There's foam seeping between her lips and a spray of food on her pillow. My hand rises to my mouth as my stomach lurches. My mother is choking on her own vomit.

I stop breathing. I don't move. The temperature in the room seems to plummet. I stand there in my dressing gown, listening to that strangled noise. Then her head tilts towards me and her bloodshot eyes open. I spring to action, turning my mother onto her side, opening her mouth and performing the disgusting task I would not wish on anyone—clearing her airway of the vile mixture clogging it.

"It's all right," I soothe. "Stay on your side now."

I hurry back to my room, pick up my phone,

and dial 999. Then I go back to Mum and watch her suck in air as though she is reborn.

There's no denying it. I hesitated again. I almost let her die.

*

I sit next to her in the white room. The brightness is blinding and unnerving. The hospital smells are making me claustrophobic and uncomfortable. The seat is hard and my back aches against the cheap plastic, but I wouldn't be able to relax anyway, not when Mum is lying wan and thin in the bed beside me. There's a tube coming from her arm, to "hydrate her", the doctors say. One of them approaches me now, holding a file and not smiling. I stand to greet her, shake her warm hand, and then step back to wrap my arms around my unsupported chest.

"Ms. Howland?" she says, emphasising the "Ms". She seems like the kind of woman who has everything together. She's probably five or six years older than I am—judging by the grey in her dark hair and the wrinkles around her eyes—but it feels like a generation. She holds herself with confidence. I imagine that she's the mother of brilliant teenagers who will ace their GCSEs in a year or two. She's the kind of woman I always assumed I'd grow up to be. Someone who doesn't get overwhelmed by bills and dating profiles. "I'm Dr. Masood. I've been taking care of your mother this morning." She glances at my pyjamas with a frown.

"My mother's carer is bringing me clothes," I explain. "It was all a blur when the ambulance came this morning."

"Quite," she says. "Well, that's good that you have help. You mother is suffering with early onset Alzheimer's disease, is that right?"

"Yes," I say. "Diagnosed a little over a year ago. She's progressing very fast. She's been quite confused lately. She has better days, though."

"I'm sorry to hear that she's progressing through the disease at such a fast pace. Unfortunately, it's not an uncommon occurrence for patients with early Alzheimer's." She pauses. "Has your mother hurt herself in any way? Or shown a desire to hurt herself?"

"No," I say. "Although I did find some bruising on her arms. She said she didn't remember how it happened. Well, that's not strictly true. She said it was a shadow. She's been mentioning it a lot, this shadow. She says it hides in her room." I try to let out a small laugh to lighten the mood, but it comes out callous.

"Right," the doctor says. She glances down at her file and then back at me. "It appears that your mother drank some bleach. It wasn't a lot of bleach, but enough to make her sick."

"She... what?"

"Sadly, patients with dementia as severe as your mother's do display strange or odd behaviour. It might not mean that she intended to hurt herself, but it could be cause for concern if anything like this happens again. You did the right thing. You acted with a cool head and saved her life. We managed to get to her before there was any permanent damage done from the bleach or from the lack of oxygen. Well done. You should be proud of yourself."

I think of that terrifying moment when I stood there and watched my mother struggle to breathe. I don't think I deserve any sort of praise. I should not feel proud. In fact, I want to throw up. I want out of this stuffy room with the flickering strip light and IV drip.

"Are you all right?" Dr. Masood asks. "You're a little pale."

"It's been quite a morning," I admit. I try to swallow, but my mouth and tongue are arid.

"Are you coping well? I know how hard it is to care for a patient with this disease." She places a hand on my shoulder and squeezes. It's a small "there, there" gesture from a no-nonsense woman. "I'll bring you some literature just in case. There are charities that can help."

I accept her help with thanks, but I can't imagine that she'll bring me anything I haven't read already.

As she leaves, she turns around and says, "Don't worry. We'll be discharging her as soon as her vitals are back up and she's rehydrated. Your mum will be home with you soon." She flashes me what I believe to be a rare smile and disappears into the long stretch of hospital corridor.

The moment she's gone, my knees fold under me. I clutch the back of the visitor's chair to steady myself. There's the tang of bile at the back of my throat, threatening to lurch out of me. My head is light, my vision blurry. My stomach roils at the realisation that the doctor thinks I'm so anxious to have Mum home when only hours ago I hesitated before helping her. I watched. It was only a fragment of time, but I watched her choke.

What kind of a person am I? What kind of a daughter? Mum has her faults, that can't be denied, but she never gave up on me, and she never abandoned me. She fed and clothed me, and now here I am doing the same for her—and I almost let her die?

I'm a monster.

EDDINGTON, 1987

The cold bites my skin the first time I pull the duvet down. My naked arms are freezing cold. Mum won't put the heating on until December. We're not made of money, she says.

"Sophie?"

I shrink back under the covers at the sound of her voice. The shrillness is a clear warning bell. She's woken up in one of her moods.

"Get up! We're going out."

I hurry out from under the covers, shivering as I rush to my drawers to pull out underwear and clothes. Her footsteps come up the stairs, each one a stark prospect as she gets nearer and nearer. I'm pulling on trousers as she bursts through the door. It's not a school day today, which comes with a unique set of difficulties. I don't need to wear a school uniform, and Mum is particular about what I wear. As soon as she's in the room, she strides over, pushes me onto the bed, and yanks the trousers down my seven-year-old legs.

"Not those ones. Here." She tosses me clothes from my drawers.

Thick woollen tights, a corduroy skirt, and a woollen jumper with a high neck.

"Mummy, they—"

"What?"

"They make me itch, Mummy."

"Nonsense. Put them on. They're your favourite clothes."

I'm almost in tears as I pull on the tights over my knickers. The roughness of the material is harsh against my sensitive skin. The outfit is too small. The crotch of the tights sags down my thighs.

Mum picks up a brush from the top of my drawers and begins to brush my hair. "There! Don't you look nice in your outfit?"

"It's too small," I say.

She pulls my hair back, and I cry out. "Stop being silly, Sophie. This is your favourite outfit. Don't you remember? You always used to wear it. Every winter, you'd wear this jumper."

"I suppose so," I say. Maybe I do remember wearing it. It does seem familiar, at least. When I stroke my fingers over the sleeves, the gesture brings with it a memory of finding strands of hair stuck to the material. Then I think of the same strands of hair caught in my fist. My stomach flips. I don't like that memory. I push it back down.

Mum tuts. "I can't do anything with this hair.

What have you done to it?"

I stay silent.

"You need to look nice. We both do. I'm meeting Roger today." She parts my hair and begins to braid the left side. "He's our key, Sophie. He's going to get us out of this mess. He's rich, you know. He's going to help us."

"But... I don't understand, Mummy. I thought Roger was your boss. How is he going to help us?" The question is innocent. I don't understand why Roger would want to help us. He has his own family to help.

Mum's hands stop moving. She tugs on the braid, pulling my head back.

"Ow! You're hurting me!"

"You're such an idiot, Sophie. You don't understand anything." She lets go of the plait and pushes me away. "He'll never help us, not when I'm burdened with an ungrateful child like you. Look at you. You're a mess. You look awful. No wonder your father left us. I bet he was trying to get away from you when he put his head through that noose. It's all your fault. If I'd never had you..."

I have tears in my eyes. Her face is bright red with anger. Her dark eyes flash. She throws the comb to the floor and stands up, clenching her fists at her sides.

"I'll just have to leave you here when I go to see him," she says. "I can't risk you messing everything up. I have to get this right, or he'll never leave his wife. There's bread in the cupboard. You can have that for your tea. Not too much, though, or you'll get fat. No one likes a fat girl."

CHAPTER SEVEN

It's in a taxi, six hours later, that I take Mum home. She's disorientated, but not agitated. The doctors have administered medication to keep her calm. I appreciate the break from her distressed state, yet at the same time I'm wary of her new impassiveness.

"Why didn't you love me like a normal mum would?" I whisper. "Why is it that all I get from you is either nastiness or nothingness?"

She can't answer me. I wonder if she ever will. I regard her, then; I study her intensely. I examine her wrinkles, the curl of her hair, the flecks in her eyes. I see the sagging chest beneath her top—a long-sleeve t-shirt brought by Erin—the thinness of her legs, the veins on her hands. I see at it all, and I remember every argument, every harsh word.

Until I scrutinise even deeper. A shiver runs up my spine. There's a niggle in the back of my mind. I stare at her, and I get the strongest feeling that she's hidden a part of my past from me. Why do I think that?

"Mum, why did you drink the bleach?" I ask.

Her eyes move in my direction, but there's only the faintest glimmer of recognition.

"Mum? Why did you drink the bleach?" I know she's in there. I know it. A woman like Maureen Howland never goes away. She's endurance itself. Even in death her spirit will be within me, criticising me, keeping me from reaching true happiness. "Tell me. Tell me why you drank it!"

Her eyes open and close as though she's trying to focus on me. Her mouth begins to move. Her hand twitches. I lean across the seat, angling my ear closer to her lips. The expelled air from her lungs wafts against the hair by my ear. I hear her trying to form the words. I hear her lick her lips and swallow, as though her throat is dry.

"Tell me," I prompt. "Tell me now."

I can't help it. The hardness is inside me. I want to be better, but my resentment towards this woman will always be there and I can't stop it. It's only the fear of her that keeps it in check. I try to love her. I've tried over and over again.

"The..." she starts.

After a pause, I prompt her again. "The what? Mum?"

"Shadow."

I sit back up straight. The driver glances up to watch us through the rear view mirror. When his eyes meet mine, he turns his head away.

"Mum, what is the shadow? You need to tell me." Again, there's that niggle at the back of my mind. Some sort of recognition. Someone from my past. But who? They're all dead, our other family members: Dad killed himself when I was four, and my grandparents never featured in my life, but they died several years ago. There's no one else. There were my mother's boyfriends, but they never lasted long. They were usually married and wealthy. We often survived by selling Mum's jewellery from past lovers. She says that's how we managed to afford to move from East London to Eddington. I'm not sure how much of that is true, though. I've never been sure where Mum got the money to move. We were so poor, we were living on bread and butter at that point. Mum worked as a cleaner. She wasn't trained for much. In Eddington, she managed to get a few jobs as a secretary or a receptionist. We struggled in a freezing cold flat for a while as she slowly saved up enough to buy a house. Roger came along at the right time. She swindled him for enough to get us on our feet.

Roger... He'd be in his sixties now. I still vaguely remember his fat hands and thick-rimmed glasses...

"Shadow," she says again. She blinks a few times, as though waking from a deep sleep. "Where are we going?"

"We're going home, Mum," I say. "Can you tell

me who the shadow is?"

"Sophie, why are you wearing that horrible outfit? I didn't raise you to not understand that you have to comb your hair in the morning."

"Mum, listen to me. Who is the shadow?"

The driver pulls onto our street. I can see the cat from across the street pooing in the front garden of three doors down.

"But where have we been? I don't understand."

"We're on our way home from the hospital. You drank some bleach and hurt yourself."

"Oh, yes, the shadow told me to do that." She nods to herself.

"But who is the shadow!"

"Sophie, don't shout. It's not ladylike. Fancy going to a hospital dressed like that. Doctors work in hospitals, you know. They earn a pretty penny. Oh, I don't want to go home. Can we stay in the car? I don't want to go into that house."

The taxi driver eyes me from the front of the car. He pulls in by the kerb. "Everything all right, love?"

"Yes," I say. "My mother has Alzheimer's disease."

He shakes his head. "I'm sorry. I went through it with an uncle. Nasty business. Five-fifty please, love."

I dig into my purse as Mum stares out at our house.

"Please, Sophie. I don't want to go in there."

The note of desperation in her voice gives me

chills. Though the Alzheimer's has rendered my mother intermittently weak, I've never heard her beg me like that. I find a five-pound note and a pound coin for the driver.

"It's going to be fine," I say, forcing cheer into my voice. "This is our house. You're safe here."

She shakes her head. "No, we're not."

I ignore the way my blood runs cold, and the way my hand shakes as I open the car door. The taxi driver tries to give me change, but I tell him to keep it. I make my way around to Mum's side and help her out. Still, she continues to stare at our house—a normal, semi-detached house on a very boring street—as though the thought of setting foot inside fills her with dread. I take her bag in one hand and her elbow in the other and guide her to the front door. She's pale as a ghost as we go inside. I close the door behind us, and we're alone in our home.

*

I'm running on empty.

I haven't quite managed to repair my relationship with Erin after accidentally accusing her of hurting Mum, but she feels sorry enough for me that she makes me a strong cup of tea the next morning. She's ten minutes early and offers a weak smile when I leave for work.

I'm exhausted from the emotionally draining day, but I have responsibilities. As hard as I try to focus on work, all throughout the morning, my mind drifts back to the conversation in the taxi. I can't stop thinking about this shadow. It's as though I'm being haunted. At lunchtime, when I tell Alisha about the weekend, she suggests I actually am haunted.

"My nana had a ghost, you know," she says. "An old man who used to stand in the corner of the guest bedroom. I saw him once. He stood there, staring, and didn't say a word."

"Are you sure it wasn't a coat hung up, or a wardrobe door left open?"

"I swear on my little boy's life that it was a ghost. I woke up in the middle of the night. My eyes adjusted to the dark. There he was, standing straight at me. He wasn't smiling. I remember the whites of his eyes like it was yesterday."

We're both on playground duty. It's a warm day but with a blustery wind. Her dark hair is whipped up around her head. She rubs her arms through her shirt.

"It frightened you," I reply.

"I nearly pissed myself, Soph. It was the single most terrifying moment of my life. I'll never forget it."

I purse my lips, quelling the desire to tell her it was probably a nightmare. There are times to correct people and times to be quiet. This is one of those times where silence is the best option. Besides, who am I to say her experience wasn't genuine? I don't believe in ghosts at all, but does that mean they don't exist? Who knows what's out there in the world intangible to humans.

"Hey, what happened to Peter?" she asks suddenly.

"I get the odd missed call from him. But not much else. Right after I deleted my profile, I received a prank call on our house phone. I assumed it was him, and it shook me up a bit. Then all this stuff happened with Mum, and I didn't really think about it anymore."

"Be careful. It's all too coincidental that your mum mentioned a shadowy figure hanging around *and* you're getting bombarded by calls from an internet weirdo. Make sure you keep your doors locked at night."

I shake my head. "It can't be anyone getting in at night. There's no sign of anyone breaking in, and I check all the windows and doors before I go to bed. I think it's a figment of Mum's imagination. It's probably the Alzheimer's."

"Do you think she's hallucinating?" Alisha tilts her head in my direction, her attention piqued. I've noticed how people's eyes glaze over when I talk about Mum's disease in general terms, but if I mention any odd or erratic behaviour, they're all ears.

"No... I don't know. The word 'shadow' is so familiar to me. I suppose it's this new context of using the word—as though I'm being followed. I get this sense of déjà vu every time I think about it, and I'm almost certain it's to do with my childhood." I take a side step to avoid a football. The kids wave at me before the regular raucous playground activities continue. "I've never known how we managed to move to Eddington when I was little. I know this doesn't seem related, but for some reason it's been on my mind a lot."

"How do you mean?"

"Well, we were dirt poor in East London. I wore the same clothes for years, even though they didn't fit. We ate bread and broth most days. Some days we went without both. Mum worked as a cleaner to pay the mortgage after Dad died without leaving us any life insurance." I pause, suppressing a shudder at the thought of those years. They're such a blur, but I can still remember the itch of the wool jumpers I layered up to stay warm in winter, and the ache in my belly when it came to dinnertime. "Then we moved to Eddington, a pretty wealthy little corner of England. For the first few years, we were as poor as we were in London. I remember the tiny flat Mum used to rent. But it was *Eddington*. The house prices are touching the sky. Even after a few years, and after Mum managed to save up somehow, we were never as well off as the rest of the people here, but we still found a small house to buy."

"She managed to find half the married men in the village, too." Alisha raises her eyebrows.

"She told me that she sold jewellery from an old boyfriend to move here. But I don't remember any boyfriends around that time, or any jewellery.

Having said that, I don't remember a lot from those days. I barely remember Dad."

"A deposit for a house was a substantial amount of money, even in those days," Alisa says.

"Exactly. So, what the hell is going on?"

The bell tolls to mark the beginning of the afternoon lessons. As always, my eyes are drawn to Chloe as she wanders into the school building alone. She's wearing a pink dress today, with white tights and black shoes. It's a little young for her, I think. It makes her stand out against the jeans and t-shirts of the other kids.

"Soph." Alisha pulls me back from my thoughts. "Take one problem at a time, yeah? Chloe has a psychologist to help her, and her parents are cooperative."

I smile. "Are my thoughts that obvious?"

"Written all over your face, love." Her expression softens and she places a hand on my shoulder. "Plus, I know you. I know that you have a soft spot for the girl. But there's too much on your mind to take on anything else. Concentrate on your mum, get through this particularly tumultuous period, and things will start to seem brighter."

"You think I'm going to get through this?"

She meets my gaze with her deep brown eyes. They're so kind, I would believe anything she says. "I know you'll get through this. You're pretty strong, you know."

We make our way towards the school. "Hey, maybe this is what you should do," she says. "You should set up some sort of recording device in your mum's room. Maybe it's not a ghost. Maybe there's a mouse in the attic or a loose floorboard. It could be frightening her so much that she's making up this shadow thing."

"You're a genius, 'Lish!"

CHAPTER EIGHT

It takes a bit of digging around in the attic to find it. I'm covered in cobwebs by the end, and my nostrils are clogged with dust. At the back of the small space is a box of Mum's old belongings. There are old clothes, broken jewellery boxes, and some notebooks she used when she was a secretary in the late eighties before computers became the norm. Right at the bottom of the box is an old jumper. I pull it out, and a few strands of light mousy-coloured hair fall from it. I pick them up and examine them.

My heart beats faster, and I toss the hair onto the attic floor. A light sweat breaks out on my forehead. What's the matter with me? They're just hairs from when I was a child. I lift up the jumper and remember its itchy feel against my skin. It seems like an odd thing for her to keep. Mum could never be accused of sentimentality. She threw away all my baby teeth, my school projects and Mother's Day gifts. Why would she keep this horrible, itchy thing made from cheap wool?

I set it aside and rummage deeper into the box. My hands find cold metal in a familiar shape. This is what I've been hoping to find. The device is in the shape of a small USB stick with a hidden microphone that can record for up to twenty hours. It was Jamie who bought it. He wanted to catch Mum out when I wasn't in the room. He tried recording her saying nasty things to him. I was gobsmacked when I found out what he'd done. I threw it in a box of old stuff and forgot all about it until my conversation with Alisha.

I slip it into my pocket and climb down the ladder onto the landing. Later, I experiment by leaving it in the kitchen as I'm making dinner for the two of us. After dinner, while Mum is sat watching her soaps, I put the USB stick into my laptop and listen to the MP3 file through a pair of headphones. There I am, chopping away, humming along to the radio. It works.

"Mum, you okay?" I call through to the living room.

"What do you want?" she snaps back. "I'm watching *Eastenders*."

"All right, Mum. I'm nipping upstairs for a shower."

There's no reply. She's probably lost in her drama by now. I collect the recording device and take it upstairs. Going into Mum's room without her there feels weird, like I'm a teenager breaking a boundary. Mum was always very private about her room, not that I ever wanted to go in there. I heard the noises that came from her room and they frightened me when I was little. First there were the strange sobs at night. Then there were the boyfriends who came for dinner and left before dawn. Now I'm older, I understand everything. I know why there were nights when she left me tucked in bed at night and didn't come home until the morning. At the time, I thought it was because she didn't love me. Perhaps it was both.

I need a good hiding place so that she won't find it, and where the microphone won't be obscured. I choose to place it behind a photograph frame on a high shelf. I can't imagine why Mum would want to look up here, so I think it should be safe. The photograph is a black-and-white picture of my grandparents and great-grandparents. They're stern and straight-backed, standing in front of a brick wall. An old dog lies at their feet, on top of what seems to be a pavement. It has to be outside some terraced house in London. The women are all boxy and tough, with their arms folded and their feet planted apart. I'm from strong stock, Mum would say. I believed her.

Perhaps I got all Dad's genes. I got his eyes. I got his habit of delving inwards and thinking too much. My only memories of him revolve around him never sticking up for us against her.

I pause.

Why would I think that?

Never sticking up for *me*.

I shake my head. I'm overtired.

The microphone is hidden. Now I wait to see what it picks up.

*

While Erin is downstairs with Mum the next morning, I remove the recording device and slip it into my handbag. There's no way I can wait until later tonight to listen to it. I'll have to find a few hours at work. There's a test I've been meaning to give the children.

"Sophie?" Erin calls from downstairs.

I hurry down the steps. "What is it?"

"There was a call, but they hung up without saying anything. Didn't you say that's happened before?" she asks.

"It's okay. I think it's that guy I met up with for a date a few weeks ago. He's been calling me a lot, too."

"What? Oh my God, is he stalking you?"

I pause. I guess I hadn't thought about it like that. Not with everything that's going on with Mum. "No, it's not stalking, is it?"

"If he's calling you, it's stalking. Does he know where you live?"

"I don't think so." I think back to our conversations online. Did I ever mention the area I live in? The street? How hard is it to track down where a person lives? I know that people who are much more competent at using Google than I am can figure things out on the internet. Maybe Peter *has* found out where I live. A cold sensation spreads over my skin. "If he figured out the phone number, maybe he figured out my address, too."

"Maybe you should go to the police," she says. "These things can escalate. Didn't your mum complain about something in the house? The shadow thing?"

My flesh crawls at the mere mention of it. "Yes, she did. Listen, don't tell Mum, but I put a recording device in her room last night. I want to make sure that there's nothing there. She's been so spooked about sleeping at night. I'm almost 90% sure that this shadow thing is her imagination running wild, but I thought I'd check."

Erin frowns. "So, you're worried too. Should I be worried about being here in the house all day? What if this Peter guy *is* stalking you?"

"If I hear anything on the recording that sounds suspicious, or if anything else happens here, I'll go to the police, I promise. And you can call me at any time and I'll come home." I glance at the time on my phone. "I'd better get to work. Call me if Mum gets agitated."

"I'm going to watch her all day," Erin promises. "I still can't believe what she did with the bleach. I know she's deteriorating, but it still seems so out of character."

Hearing her say it only highlights the grim

reality of the situation. Mum is losing her mind. She's coming undone, and her character is slowly slipping away. She's nothing like the person she used to be.

"I'll see you later. Bye, Mum." I wave to her, but she's lost somewhere in her mind, staring out of the kitchen window.

"Bye, Becca."

"That's a new one," I say with a laugh.

"Sophie, not Becca," Erin says, pronouncing each word as though she's teaching a child to spell.

"That's what I told them. They got it wrong, and I paid for it." Mum shakes her head.

I bite back tears as I leave the house. Now she doesn't even know who I am.

*

A collective groan swells across the room.

"It's a two-hour test," I tell the children, raising my voice over the squeaking of chairs, the shuffling of pencils, the whispers between friends. "And it's only going over all the subjects we've covered so far."

"But, Miss, it's boring," exclaims Noah. There are smudges of mud on his face again. No amount of sending him to the bathroom to clean up actually seems to work.

"It'll help you for your test at the end of the year." It's not strictly a lie, but I have tested them more than is necessary so far this year. I usually throw in a lot more practical activities and, well, fun lessons, but I'm itching to listen to the file from the recording device. I can only get through two hours at work, and then the rest I'll have to listen to while I'm at home.

"We hate tests, Miss." A tall boy called Sam puts his head in his hands dramatically. Kids can be very dramatic over the most ridiculous things.

"I don't hate tests." Alice has a smug smile on her haughty little face. I know I *shouldn't* dislike her, but...

"All right, that's enough, everyone. Settle down, now." The longer they faff around, the longer it will take for me to sit down and listen to the MP3 file. I raise my hands for silence before quickly handing around the materials for the test.

With the children finally organised, I pull the recording device out of the top drawer of my desk, where I put it for safekeeping while taking the register. I open my laptop and place the USB stick into the correct port. Noah is the first to look up at the noise. He watches me put the headphones on with interest. I shoot him a hard stare, and he gets back to his work. Chloe was the only child not to react to the news of the test today. Instead she scribbled in her notebook and giggled to herself. I had to turn away, repeating what Alisha had said to me. It's not my place. I can't get involved.

I play the file. Before I left for work, I managed to find the part of the recording where Mum was going to bed. I fast-forwarded to a few moments after I'd helped her into bed and left her alone. That's what starts when I click on play.

There's silence. Then a small sigh, followed by the sound of bedsheets moving. I imagine her trying to get comfortable, rolling from one side of the bed to the other. I can see the floral sheets in my mind, and her dry, dyed hair spreading across the pillow. I can see the lump of her body beneath the duvet, and the pastel pink cushioned headrest. The classroom has almost completely disappeared. I'm there.

Bowing my head over a pile of marking, I raise the volume a few bars to make sure I don't miss anything. I need to be certain that I hear everything that went on in that room. With horror, I realise that I'm excited. The anticipation of listening into my mother's private life is almost delicious. I'm enjoying this. After years of her blocking me out of my life, of watching her sneak around with married men and keep secrets from me, I'm finally getting an insight into a part of her life I know nothing about. But what sort of insight will it be? A seven-hour recording of her snoring all night?

As the time goes on, and the file remains silent except for the odd sound of Mum shifting in her sleep, or snoring, I begin to lose that excitement. Instead, I actually start marking the work in front of me, with the sound of the file merely background noise. The children yawn, stretch, and scribble across their pages. I find my attention shifting to Chloe, who is bent over her work, but moving her pencil in circles rather than writing.

Impatience begins to grasp me. I only have forty-five minutes until break time. When I set the recording, I told myself I would listen to it all. But maybe I don't need to. It was in the early hours of the morning when Mum came into my room, frightened. Perhaps I can fast-forward the file to about 2am. I work out what time I put Mum to bed, and what time I went to bed myself, then I fast-forward the file a number of hours until I think it's about 2am. Then I click play.

Still nothing.

I answer a question from a student and go back to my marking. Noah's homework has an orange mark on it that I can only assume came from a glass of orange juice or squash. I write him a note in the margin reminding him to take pride in his work.

Chloe hasn't completed the assignment. Instead, she's drawn a girl in her book. I examine the girl and wonder if it's Jessie, her imaginary friend. It's hard to work out, because the illustration resembles Chloe herself. They both have long hair pulled into a ponytail. The girl in the drawing wears a skirt similar to the one Chloe is wearing now and has a rucksack the same shape.

There's a tug at my stomach. I want to help this child. But are my desires to help her selfless or selfish? Am I projecting onto this young girl because all I've ever wanted is a daughter? I've longed to read to a child, to teach her how to spell, to go on walks into the countryside and point out beautiful flowers.

The ticking time bomb of that sexist metaphor the "biological clock" has slowed right down. It's time to accept that motherhood will probably never happen for me. And maybe that's okay. Maybe that's what was supposed to happen.

I switch up the volume. Still nothing. Only fifteen minutes to go until break. Noah wants to use the bathroom now. I roll my eyes and nod. I move onto the next exercise book.

And then I hear it.

"What are you doing here?"

The sound makes me jolt. I quickly turn down the volume a few bars. Some of the kids turn to stare at me, so I put my head down and pretend to mark.

The voice is my mother's. But who is she speaking to?

"Tell me what you're doing here. I want to know."

There's a pause, a long, agonising, pregnant pause. Silence.

"I... I..." Mum stutters. "I know you..."

The thud of my heart is almost audible. The nerves and anticipation feel like bugs crawling under my skin. There's a creeping feeling of nausea rising from the pit of my stomach. I want an answer, and yet I don't want an answer. My fingers hover over the mousepad, trembling. I can't breathe.

"*You will know me.*"

A scream rips from my body.

CHAPTER NINE

Alisha bursts into the classroom. There are children crying on the back row. Noah stares at me with his jaw dropped. My fingers grip the seat of my chair, and I attempt to suck in deep breaths that rasp through my lungs. Alisha runs towards me, blurry and frantic. I try to tell her about the upset children, but I'm paralysed by the beating of my heart. It's so loud I think it might burst.

"It's on the recording." I finally find my voice. "It's on the recording."

Alisha lifts one of my arms, examines me. "Are you hurt? What's wrong? Breathe, Sophie, breathe."

I can barely hear her over the voice in my head. *You will know me. You will know me.* That harsh whisper sets my teeth on edge. My heart pounds against my ribs, threatening to come out of my chest, burst forth and escape. I wouldn't blame it. I would jump ship too if I was part of this broken woman. I'm a mess. A complete and utter mess.

"It's all right, children. Miss Howland isn't feeling well right now. You can go into my classroom if you like. Go on, that's right." Alisha's hair brushes over my hand when she leans down to me. "Jesus, Sophie, come on. Pull yourself together. You're at school, teaching children." She pats my hand.

I feel sick.

*

Moira sends me home, citing exhaustion. They wanted to call an ambulance but I wouldn't let them. No, I need to get home. I need to see that room, to imagine the voice again, to feel what's real and what's not. And I need to make sure Mum and Erin are safe.

I have no idea who was in the room with Mum. The voice is so low and hoarse that it could be male or female. On the way home in the car, I put my laptop on the passenger seat and listen to it again. After the whisper, Mum makes a few whimpering sounds, but then seems to ease back into sleep. I wonder if she even remembers it.

You will know me.

You will know me.

I keep playing it over and over in my mind.

She *knew* the person in her room. She's never met Peter, so it can't be him. It could be anyone she used to know. Anyone from her past. Perhaps it's someone I've never met before.

The shadow.

Why didn't I take her seriously? How long has this person been breaking into our house at night?

How did they get in?

The nape of my neck prickles as the memory comes back to me. *I can't find my keys.* Mum lost her keys not long ago and then found them the next morning. What if they were stolen from her, taken overnight, and the thief made a copy? Erin said Mum had been out in the garden that day. That was the night I found the button.

I pull sharply onto my road, narrowly missing the neighbour's cat. Handbrake up. Seatbelt unclipped. I rush towards the house. My frenetic fingers miss the keyhole twice before I open the door. When I burst into the hallway, I catch a glimpse of the wild woman in the mirror, shambolic and undone, all pink-faced and bloodshot.

"Sophie?" Erin's soft footsteps patter through the house. "Is that you?"

I meet her halfway, almost running into her in the living room doorway. Her eyes widen in fear at the sight of me.

"Has anyone been in the house? Have you noticed anyone hanging around?" I ask.

Her pretty eyes are like plates, and her mouth makes an "O" shape. "No, no one has been. What's happened?"

I'm breathless. My trembling hand rises to my chest. I need to pull myself together if I'm going to handle this. "Alisha... I..." I take a deep breath and compose myself. "With Mum saying that there was a shadow in her room, I decided to put a recording device in there. It was Alisha's idea. She said there might be a mundane explanation for Mum's fear that I could record. So, I recorded her room at night and then listened to the file while I was at work. Erin, *there was someone in the house.*"

Her hand rises to her mouth, stifling a gasp. "What?"

"I heard them. I heard their voice on the recording. I'm going to call the police."

Erin nods. "Good."

"Do you remember the day Mum lost her keys? You said she'd been in the garden."

"Yes, that's right." She lowers her head as though reliving the day. Then her head snaps up. "It wasn't long after she came inside that she said she'd lost them. We searched all over the garden, but they weren't there. I remember she was playing with them that day, walking around and jangling them up and down. It seemed to keep her occupied, so I left her to it."

"Did Mum say anything about seeing someone in the garden?"

"No." Erin scratches the back of her neck. "No, and I didn't see anyone."

I rummage through my bag, looking for my mobile phone. "On the recording, it sounds like she knew the person who broke into the house. I'm almost certain of it."

Erin wraps her arms around her body. "I get chills just thinking about it." Then she pauses. "What time was the person in the house?"

"Sometime after 2am. About 2:45, I think. Why?"

"Well, it could be nothing, but…"

"Go on," I prompt.

"Sometimes your mum takes a nap in the afternoon. When she wakes up, she's very disorientated. She'll stare at her reflection in the window and say things like, 'What are you doing here?' and 'Do I know you?' If it was the middle of the night and she'd just woken up, she could have said that to anyone."

"So, it could have been anyone?"

That's when it hits me. If the intruder could have been anyone, that means I can't trust anyone. I turn away from Erin with the phone in my hand. Erin has more access to Mum's keys than anyone. Maybe I can't trust her, either.

*

PC Hollis and PC Chowdhury are polite but serious. Hollis is older, with grey stubble, a wide jaw and a boxer's physique. He resembles the kind of police officer you see on TV. The good cop who works with the maverick. Chowdhury is leaner and has small, dark eyes that can't rest in one spot. He sits quietly as Hollis leads the investigation. His only reaction is to the recording, when his eyebrows lift up his forehead.

"Did you hear it?" I ask eagerly. "The voice?"

"Ms. Howland, may I ask why you decided to put a recording device in your mother's bedroom?" PC Hollis asks. The masculine energy of the two officers seems out of place sat on my mother's floral sofa sipping from chintzy teacups.

"Mum has Alzheimer's disease," I explain. "She gets disorientated and confused at night. Her sleep has been very disrupted, and she keeps complaining about a shadow following her. Which I know sounds a bit crazy." I let out a nervous laugh and feel my skin heat with embarrassment. "I was worried that she was frightening herself at night somehow. I didn't expect this. I didn't expect to actually hear an intruder."

Chowdhury makes notes. Hollis asks, "And what about you, Ms. Howland? Did you hear anyone come into the house last night?"

"No," I reply. "I didn't. But a few nights ago, Mum woke me up and said there was someone in her room. We checked the whole house, but we didn't find anything."

"And you didn't hear anything that night, either?" Hollis asks.

"No," I reply as a prickling sensation works its way up my arms. It wasn't until the police started asking questions that I realised how odd all this is. "But Mum lost her keys. The intruder could have made a set. I guess I might not hear someone sneak into the house if they can unlock the door."

"Maybe I should take a look around," Chowdhury suggests. "Do you have a cellar or an attic?"

"Yes, both," I say. My blood runs cold. "You don't think... you don't think they're still here, do you?"

"Don't worry," Chowdhury says with a reassuring smile. "If there's anyone here, we'll find them."

"Perhaps I could have a chat with your mother while PC Chowdhury searches the house?" Hollis suggests.

"Yes, I'll go and get her."

I direct Chowdhury towards the cellar, making sure the light is on so he doesn't slip down the steep stone steps. As with most old Victorian houses, the cellar is cold and uninviting, where the meat would have been stored to keep it fresh. There's even an old stone butcher's block down there. Not that I go into the cellar very often. I have to build up the courage to go down there to change a fuse.

Mum is in the kitchen with Erin, who seems frazzled as she wards off many questions. *Who are those men? What are they doing in my house?* As I walk into the room, Mum turns around and directs the same questions at me.

"It's the police, Mum. They want to talk about the person who broke into the house. Do you remember? You need to tell them all about it."

Mum's face drains of all colour. "But I don't want to. I don't want to tell them." She takes a step forward and whispers, "They mustn't know. Never."

"Mum... What? I..." I glance across at Erin, who is chewing on her lip and tapping nervously on the kitchen surface. She turns away, busying herself with washing mugs. "What are you talking about?"

But the spell is broken. Mum leans away from me and blinks twice. "Who are those men in my house?"

For the briefest of moments, I wonder... Is Mum as confused as she seems? When she regards me with those assessing eyes, it's as though she knows what she's saying. Then her jaw slackens, and I wonder if I saw anything at all.

I guide her through to the living room—where PC Hollis is waiting for us—and feel numb from head to toe. Numb, and tired of all this. My mind drifts to my class at school, being taught by Alisha again. I can't help experiencing a stab of jealousy. Alisha gets to teach my kids. She also has the home life I've always wanted. I'm here with the police, a demented mother, and a sick feeling in my stomach.

Hollis gets to his feet and offers a hand to shake. Mum stands with her back straight. She never even glances at his hand. Instead, she folds her arms and lifts her chin.

"What is all this nonsense about?" she demands.

"Mrs. Howland, your daughter called us about an intruder. You said that there was someone in your bedroom? There's a recording—"

"I don't like you being in my home."

"Mum! I'm very sorry. It's the Alzheimer's, not her," I lie.

"That's okay. I don't like the police in my home, either," Hollis says with a laugh. "But we're here to help, Mrs. Howland. I know this is all quite distressing. Perhaps we should listen to the MP3 file that your daughter recorded. Maybe it will jog your memory."

"File? What's an MP3?"

I swallow through a dry throat. My hands are clammy against my hips. "Mum, I put a recording device in your bedroom because of what you said about the intruder. I know I should have told you, but I wanted to make sure you were all right at night. You've been so disrupted recently."

"You recorded me?"

I cringe away from her, and Hollis shuffles his feet and stares down at the mug of tea on the coffee table. No one wants to gaze at Maureen Howland's wide, frightening eyes, accusing me of a hundred crimes. Crime one: betrayal.

"I thought—"

"You disgust me."

Hollis clears his throat. "Maybe we should discuss the intruder. There is a voice on the file that does sound like a second person. Mrs. Howland, do you remember talking to someone in your room

103

late at night? Did they hurt or threaten you?"

Mum sits down in the armchair and stares vacantly out of the window. "I don't know what you're talking about. I don't remember."

Hollis clicks play on the laptop and the whole ordeal is played again. Mum's only reaction to the voice is to turn and stare at the computer as though it called her name.

"Mrs. Howland, is this your voice?" Hollis replays the first part of the recording.

"Yes," Mum replies.

"And what about this voice?" He plays the hiss that makes my knees weaken with fear.

Mum shakes her head. "I don't remember. I don't know anything about all this."

"Take your time, Mum," I coax.

"You don't talk to me." Mum's words cut me to the bone.

Hollis carries on the interview, ignoring the icy atmosphere. He asks her whether she saw anything strange, whether there had been any sign of a break-in, and whether anyone had been hanging around the street recently. Mum doesn't know anything. My hopes begin to dwindle. Someone *was* here, but without Mum coherent enough to tell us who it was, the police can't do anything to help us.

I decide to ignore her request. "What about the shadow? Tell them about the shadow."

"There's nothing to tell," she snaps. "I suppose it's what I think I see when I'm confused. I want to go for a lie-down now."

"There's a policeman having a look around the house at the moment, Mum. You can have a lie-down when he's done." I flash PC Hollis an apologetic smile, and his return is the sympathetic version.

The sound of boots on carpet interrupts us. PC Chowdhury breaks the tension in the room with a breezy entrance. "I've checked the cellar and upstairs, but there's nothing unusual there."

"I'll show you the attic," I say. Serial killers always hide in the attic. A shiver runs down my spine.

"Don't get lost up there." Mum's voice is laced with sarcasm. Then she laughs.

CHAPTER TEN

PC Chowdhury is nice about it, but even as we're walking up the attic steps, I get the strongest feeling that no one is there and no one has been there. I think he knows this whole thing is ridiculous as well. I begin to wonder about the recording and the implications of its contents. As I watched the two police officers listen to it, I figured that their raised eyebrows and intakes of breath were out of shock that there was an intruder in my home. Now I wonder if it was disbelief. Maybe they think I'm a crazy woman who doctored the file. Or maybe they think it was Mum.

As I stand under the single light bulb in the attic, I replay the voice in my mind. I don't need the file. I know exactly what that voice sounds like. I know every nuance and tone in that serpent-like hiss. I know every word. *You will know me.*

Could it be her?

Could it be Mum?

The stifling attic air suffocates me, and the back of my neck dampens with sweat. What if Mum spoke on the recording to frighten me? What if all of this is a cruel joke? I want to be able to dismiss that thought, but I can't. This could be her revenge. It would be just like her. She wants to make me crazier than she is because she hates me that much. My hand moves up my chest to circle my throat. I think of her, and I squeeze until I can't breathe.

"I think I'm all done."

My hand drops, and I blink my thoughts away. PC Chowdhury turns to me with a pitying smile on his face. I want to slap it off, but I settle for forming a fist at my side.

"There's nothing here," he says with a shrug. "Did your mum remember anything?"

I shake my head.

"That's a shame. She could have helped us a great deal."

He bends his head as he steps over the junk strewn around the attic floor. I finally manage to move my feet, directing him back towards the steps. He descends first. I glance back at the attic. There's nothing here, only all our junk collected over the years. Old photo albums, boxes of winter clothes, my university work. I switch off the bulb and follow Chowdhury back downstairs.

*

The police are kind enough to open an investigation, but by the time they leave, I'm already doubting what I heard on the recording. They tell me to keep a log of anything unusual and to write down, or print out records, of all inappropriate phone calls. The words make me shiver. That's what you do when you're being stalked and harassed. Stalked women never have a happy ending in the movies.

I'm not taking any chances. My next phone call is to the locksmith to change our locks. Mum hovers around the locksmith after he arrives, breathing over his shoulder and staring as he works. I barely have the energy to distract her away from him. She's confused for the rest of the day. She seems to forget all about the police coming to our home and asks me why the man is changing our locks over half a dozen times.

I answer her questions and make cups of tea. I do it all in a daze. My body is disconnected from my mind as I step around the kitchen like a zombie. Erin leaves with relief spread all over her face and with a limp wave I see through the window. The locksmith hurries out of the door, also relieved to be away from the demented old lady with the slack face and the funny questions.

And life goes on despite this little interruption. We eat dinner in relative silence, wittering to each other about mundane things like the weather and the tasteless food on our plates. We go to bed at the same time. We lie down on our beds in our separate rooms and we pretend that everything is normal.

But it isn't. Either someone was in our house, Mum is deliberately trying to drive me insane, or the Alzheimer's has her confused enough to make up voices in the night. None of those options bring me any comfort.

My dreams are as unfocused as my mind. They swim and swirl. I hear voices. *The* voice. Doors open and shut in my mind. A shadowy hand floats along the walls of our house, turning the walls into a dark, chalky substance, like ashes.

I call Alisha and Moira when I wake up, and they agree that I need another day off to recuperate from the events of yesterday. I explain what happened and they're very sympathetic about the intruder, expressing the right amount of concern and alarm. For some reason it doesn't feel genuine. Not even from Alisha, my best friend and the person I considered my only ally in this world.

The problem with finding that the world is imploding around you, and that your life has turned into a series of problems, is that there comes a time when the people around you are sick of hearing about it but are too polite to tell you they're sick of it. You're the bore who makes their day a little less sunny. You're a negative influence in their lives and there's nothing you can do about it, unless you want to keep your mouth shut and not say anything. No one wants to be the bore. When you're not it, you avoid the bore like the plague.

Then, one day, it comes around and it's you and you're alone.

I make one more phone call before breakfast. It's to Erin, telling her to take the day off. I want to spend quality time with Mum to process the events of the last few days. At least, that's what I tell her. Then I check my bank balance online and make a few phone calls. It's time to make some changes around here.

Mum is quiet, which is good. I make her tea and toast and suggest she gets some rest after what happened. She waddles off to the living room to read her book as the doorbell goes.

I answer the door to a skinny chap in blue overalls.

"You called about setting up the security system?" he asks.

"That's right. Come in."

He glances down at a piece of paper in his hand. "So, it's CCTV on the outside of the house and the nanny cameras in every room."

He doesn't say what he's thinking. But I answer the question anyway. "My mother has Alzheimer's disease, and I want to keep an eye on her while I'm at work."

"Oh," he says, apparently relieved that there's a normal explanation for my security needs.

I don't tell him that I want to watch my mother, or that I want to watch my mother's nurse, too. I don't tell him that I don't trust anyone anymore. Instead, I join Mum in the living room so I can keep her distracted while he works in the rest of the house.

When he's done with the upstairs, I suggest to Mum that we have a clothes sort-out. If there's one thing that ignites the sparkle in her eyes, it's the opportunity to criticise and throw out my clothes. She's more than willing to sit on the bed as I hold up dress after top after skirt and she tells me which body part they emphasise. Some make my ankles look fat. Others highlight my wide hips or my chubby upper arms. By the time the security guy is done, I've packed up two fat bags of clothes for a cancer charity.

"Don't forget to put them on the step," Mum says as I begin to leave the room. "The collection is tomorrow." She points to the label on the bag to demonstrate.

I swallow my snappy reply and head downstairs. The security guy is already packing up his bag.

"Are you all done? I'm sorry I completely forgot to make you a cup of tea," I say.

"No worries. I'm more of a juice drinker, anyway." He passes me a booklet. "Everything you need to know should be in here. My number is on the front, in case you need anything."

I thank the man and show him the way out of the house. When the door has closed behind him, I can't help but wonder whether I've done the right thing. Have I crossed a line? If Mum or Erin find out about this, I could burn my bridges as quickly as a forest fire. But when I examine things deeper, I can't help but wonder whether either relationship is particularly strong anyway.

When Mum's footsteps sound on the stairs, I slip the booklet into the top drawer of the cabinet and try not to stare at the hidden cameras. No, I think, I need to establish order in this house. I need to get to the bottom of whatever is going on. I'm not overreacting. This has to be done, even if I have to spend money on an expensive security system to do it.

"Was there someone in the house?" Mum asks.

"No," I reply.

"But I heard—"

"There was no one here. Was there, Mum?"

For once, she's the one who shrinks away from me. She's the one who stands there with her mouth flapping open and shut. She's the vulnerable one.

*

It's a relief to have Erin back. A full day with Mum, especially with everything going on, can be taxing. I'm more than happy to hand things over to her and head to the school. But Erin walks in through the door with a puzzled frown on her face. She leaves the front door open and gestures for me to follow her.

"I don't know what's happened, but..." She points down to the driveway.

"What the hell?"

Our drive is covered in the clothes I left out for the charity last night. I bend down and pick up one of the bags.

"It's ripped open," I say. "As though someone has pulled the plastic wrapper apart."

Erin bends down next to me. "Are you sure it wasn't clawed or chewed open by an animal?"

I'm no expert on animal tracks, but I would expect a bag to be shredded by an animal, not pulled open like this. I collect a blue blouse from amidst the gravel—a top Mum said revealed my "bingo wings". It's cut open. Slit from top to bottom.

I turn to Erin. "Do animals have scissors?"

"Fucking hell, Soph."

We remain there, staring at the clothes strewn over the ground. A few weeks ago, I would have chalked this up to bored teenagers, but now I'm not so sure. My head swims with possibilities.

I really am being stalked. But by whom? Peter is the first name who pops into my mind. He's the one who has been calling me. But what about the other people in my life? Erin? Alisha? The woman across the street with the cat? My boss, Moira? My ex-boyfriend, Jamie?

Mum. Mum faking the extent of her illness, teasing me by mentioning a shadow, pretending to see people at night, making that terrible voice on the MP3 file... All of it to punish me.

I finally come out of my trance and snap a few photographs with my phone. I'll need to keep this in my log of "unusual activity" to show the police. Then I hurriedly collect my clothes, shoving them into the ripped plastic bags, ignoring the extent of the damage. It makes me sick to my stomach to think of anyone deliberately waiting until night time, then bringing a pair of scissors and cutting through my clothes.

Then I remember. The camera.

My heartbeat quickens.

"I'm late for work."

"I can finish up here," Erin says. "I'm sorry this happened. I just don't understand it. Why would anyone do this?"

I fold my arms across my body, flinching at the reminder of how creepy this situation is. How violating it feels. "Be careful today. Keep the doors locked, okay? Whoever this is only seems to come at night, but you never know."

"You be careful too," she says. The early morning sun highlights the fine hair on her skin. She runs a hand through her pixie cut. "They could be following you."

I hurry to my car, wanting nothing more than to leave this house.

CHAPTER ELEVEN

"Sophie, how are you?"

In my haste to get to my classroom, I almost walk straight past Alisha. She frowns when she sees me, a telling testament to how frazzled I must appear. I run the back of my hand over my forehead, smearing sweat across my skin. My left arm is filled with books and my laptop. My shoulder bag is hanging from my arm. I daren't glance down at my clothes. Did I even iron them this morning? I can't remember.

"Much better, thanks." I force a smile.

Alisha does not seem convinced. Her frown only deepens, and a furrow appears between her eyebrows. Either she's worried, or she's disgusted at my dishevelled appearance.

"Are you sure? You seem stressed. Want to get a cuppa in the teacher's room? We have ten minutes until registration."

It pains me to see the hopeful expression in her eyes. I love Alisha. She's my best friend. But there will always be a barrier between us, a wall that I keep failing to pull down. It's jealousy. I'm jealous of her life, of her husband and her children, and the fact that she doesn't have a bitter, slowly decaying mother to care for. Right now I'm the bitter one, because I have to go into my classroom, plug in my laptop and watch security camera footage to find out if that same decaying woman ripped open my bag of clothes and cut them into ribbons to spite me, because she hates her own daughter so much.

"I can't, sorry, I have marking to do." My tone is brusque and unfair. I'm walking away from her as she stands staring after me. All she ever does is try to help me, and I can't find a way to be grateful. It hurts to be around her while my life is falling to pieces. It hurts to be around anyone happy, because I see the way I suck the happiness from the room.

It's a relief to open the door to my classroom, and a relief to close it behind me. I dump the books on my desk and quickly set up my laptop. I don't have a lot of time, and I've got a complicated system to work out. I spent most of last night reading and rereading the booklet I received with the installation.

I log in and pull up the camera feed from the front of the house. It takes me a couple of attempts, but soon I'm able to rewind the feed and play short busts through the night, rewinding and fast-forwarding until I find activity on the recording. There's the neighbour's cat again; a fox comes sniffing up to the bag and I freeze, wondering if my paranoia was just that... but then the fox turns away and runs into the night.

It's not until about 4am that there's movement again. It's so quick that I almost miss it. I rewind and watch again. It's almost a blur.

A figure darts from the hedge on the left of the screen towards our door. Then it disappears. I catch my breath, try to calm my heart, and watch again. The figure is almost completely in shadow and little more than a black blob in the darkness. But, despite its being hunched over, it's almost certainly a person. The problem is, the person disappears directly underneath the camera, which is affixed to the wall above the door. They must be crouched down next to the step where the charity bag is still sitting.

I keep watching the recording. For almost thirty seconds, nothing happens. Then I start as a gloved hand reaches out and snatches the bag of clothes. The sickness in my stomach rises to my throat. I clamp a hand over my mouth to keep it down. I need to keep a clear head. I need to watch the rest of this recording and find out exactly who is stalking me and why. But there's little else to see. At one point, some of my clothes fly up into the air, making me gasp. I'm watching a person destroy my things for no apparent reason. More of my clothes are thrown into the air, and then there's another blur and the vandal is gone.

I sit back in my chair, covered in cold sweat, defeated and drained. I was so convinced that this would show that Mum was playing a cruel joke. Instead, I know no more than I did yesterday. The figure was so hunched, and moved so fast, that it could have been anyone. I didn't even assess their physique. They could be fat or thin, male or female.

The children begin to filter into the classroom as I start to watch the footage from Mum's room in fast-forward. About two hours in, the camera goes blank. I pause the feed and try to rewind it.

"Miss, are you going to do registration? Shall I do it for you?" Alice being a goody two-shoes again.

I pick up my register and read out the names of the students, but all the time—even as I'm marking ticks next to their names—all I can think about is the video feed. Why did it go blank? Could Mum have figured out what I've done? Did she turn the camera off somehow? And if she did, how did she do it without walking up to the camera? I would have seen her do it. Perhaps the camera is faulty. The timing is disastrous, but these things do happen.

It's a struggle, but I force my concentration back to the children. It's not their fault so much is going on in my private life. They still deserve an education. So, for the entire morning, that's what they get. There are moments where I find myself zoning out, thinking about the stalker, about the clothes and about Mum, but I manage to be coherent enough to stick to the lesson plan. But as soon as it's over, I'm back to my laptop watching the footage. The footage from Mum's camera is completely blank for the rest of the night. I give up on it, instead switching to the live feed in the rest of the house. It jolts me for a moment. I didn't quite expect the feeling of shame that washes over me as I watch Erin in the kitchen heating up soup for Mum as she sits at the table. It's so intimate. So voyeuristic. And oddly compelling.

Erin appears to be chatting, while Mum sits stoically still. When Erin takes the soup across to the table, Mum is scowling. She folds her arms and turns away while Erin patiently places the bowl before her, with the spoon on the right. Erin sits down next to Mum with her sandwich, smiling brightly. But Mum is still scowling. Eventually she picks up the spoon and drops it into the bowl. The soup splatters over the table, and I'm still sat staring at them, watching the stubbornness of my mother as she refuses to eat. Erin even offers the woman her own sandwich, but still Mum looks away.

I'm so enthralled in the video feed that I hardly notice the children come back. I missed playground duty altogether. My face burns with embarrassment. I can't remember who I was supposed to work with on playground duty. Maybe it was Samuel, the one male teacher on our staff, an older man with grey nose hair and a tea-spotted tie. I rub my eyes with the heels of my hands, failing to rub away the thoughts from my mind.

The rest of the afternoon is a diluted version of my lesson plan. I let the children get way out of hand during their individual work while I watch more of Erin and Mum going about their day. I see nothing out of the ordinary on the video feed. Mum is her usual stubborn self, nearly always sitting or standing with her arms folded, her chin high and haughty. Erin spends most of the time chatting, all smiles and patience. I can't hear what she's saying, but I imagine it's the same kind of chatter I hear when I'm with them, comments on the weather or compliments on Mum's outfit, anything breezy and light.

At the end of the day I have no desire to stop and chat with my colleagues, and I definitely want to avoid Moira, so I pack up my things and rush to my car.

The summer weather appears to be breaking. Dark clouds have formed above. The air is thick with a pre-storm atmosphere. My skin is slick with sweat from the muggy climate. At these times, when the weather changes so quickly, I no longer feel like I'm in England. I miss the grey drizzle of two-thirds of the year. This dramatic atmosphere belongs in an exotic country far from here. I want the comfort of my homeland back. I want a soggy umbrella and damp feet, not a pressure that makes my sinuses ache.

I want things to be normal again.

I run my fingers through my hair and take a deep breath.

*

PC Hollis promises to watch the video footage from the front of the house. But I know he won't find anything significant about the shadowy figure appearing from the hedge. I check the camera in Mum's room to find that a wire has come loose at the back. Then I email the security guy, who can't fix it for another week. So I swap Mum's camera with another while she's taking a bath.

I have a few more calls from Peter on my phone. I take screenshots of each one for my log. I had hoped he'd got bored of me and moved on to someone else, but it seems he's harder to shake than that.

It's late by the time I finally stop moving. I sink into bed and fall into a deep slumber, dreaming of walking outside to find Mum hunched over the bag of clothes. Her head jerks to the left, like a startled animal's. I take a step forward, holding out my hand as I would with a wild deer or a frightened horse. She rips open the bag and lifts out one of my shirts. I can only watch as she places the cuff of the shirt in her mouth and begins to chew.

"Stop it!" I cry.

But she keeps on chewing on my shirt until saliva drips down her chin.

I take a step back, horrified at the sight, when another figure appears from the hedge. There's nothing about the figure that's recognisable as a person. It's a shadow, devoid of features, but it seems so familiar. Ignoring Mum, I step towards the shadow, but my head is ripped back.

I wake up with a start, sitting bold upright in bed. My alarm is blaring out. As I reach out to turn it off, I notice that my hand is clasped tight. When I open my fist, tiny flecks of brown scatter from my fingers.

Strands of hair. My hair.

I leap out of bed and examine the mattress. There is a clump of hair strewn across the bed and a patch of drying blood on my pillow. Slowly, dreading what I know I'll find, and with a numb feeling spreading over my flesh, I lift my hand to the back of my head. When I find it, I let out a little gasp. Blood. I stare down at the hair in my hand with disbelief washing over me. Am I really so crazy that I'm ripping my own hair out of my head? In my sleep?

And yet... there's something... so familiar about seeing hair in my hand. I close my fingers and make a fist, and as I do, I get the strongest sensation of déjà vu, that at some point in my life I've done this before.

"Will you turn off that alarm!" Mum bustles into the room, breaking the spell. She snatches my phone from the bedside table and thrusts it into my hand. "Deal with it!"

With shaking fingers I slide the bar across the screen to turn off the alarm. Then I turn and regard my mother.

She shakes her head. "Sort yourself out." And walks out of the room.

I hurry to the mirror to examine the damage to my hair. Luckily, I pulled most of the hair from the back of my head, and the bleeding has already stopped. If I can wash my hair and get a plaster on the cut, I can tie my hair back and cover up the issue.

I drop the dead hair onto my nightstand and stare at it one more time. What am I forgetting?

The thought of my unconscious self ripping the hair from my head haunts me in the shower and even as I make breakfast. Every slight sound jolts me from unsettled thoughts. The toaster is a gunshot. The scrape of a chair is an intruder. My toes are kissing the knife edge, and I can't see my way down.

When I greet Erin at the door, I expect to be soothed by her presence. Instead, I find a withdrawn woman with smudged makeup and red eyes. She barges past me into the hallway without even saying hello.

"I'm only doing today," she announces.

"What do you mean? What's happened?"

She yanks her jacket from her body, which is damp from the rain that finally began in the early hours of this morning. "I don't know how you have the gall to ask me that."

"I... I don't understand—"

"You made it perfectly clear in the email. I don't understand how you could have accused me of anything like that. I take *good* care of your mum. I've never done anything... I... I thought we were friends—"

"Erin, slow down. Tell me what you think I've done."

"There's no point denying it," she says. "I know you didn't mean to send it to me, but you did. We're done, Sophie. I'll work today because I know you can't find another nurse on such short notice, but tomorrow you need to find someone else. I'm sorry, but I've made up my mind. I can't work with someone who would stab me in the back like that."

Before I can respond, she strides into the kitchen and slams the door behind her, leaving a clear signal for me to leave her alone. And I'm late for work. But on my way out, I check my email account to figure out what she could be talking about. There, in the sent items, is an email from my account going to Erin and her boss, with the subject: *Erin Jones is abusing my mother.*

EDDINGTON, 1997

"This is good work, Sophie." Mrs. Vaughan hands me back my essay and straightens up, stretching her back. She's always doing that. Every now and then she warns us "young 'uns" that we should maintain good posture or we'll end up with bad backs when we're old. Like her. "We need to talk to you about university."

I stare down at my desk, hoping that no one notices the flush working up my neck. Even though the rest of the class is busy with their own work, my scalp prickles with the sensation that they are all watching me.

"Oh, I won't be applying to university." The words seem awkward and clumsy. I pull on my sleeves, hiding my hands. I don't want to have this conversation, not now. Why did I open my mouth?

Mrs. Vaughan shifts her weight from one foot to the other and folds her arms, crushing the rest of her papers against her chest. "What do you mean?"

"I can't afford to move away." Again, I feel eyes on me. I want to shrink into the ground, or at least somehow get Mrs. Vaughan to stop talking.

"But you can apply for a grant," she continues. "Don't worry, I can show you how. I can help you fill out all the paperwork, if you like." She pauses as I struggle for another reply. "Hold on. I'll find a pamphlet."

I stare down at the circled "A" on the top right-hand corner of my essay, wondering how I'm going to explain to Mrs. Vaughan that there's no way my mother will let me go to university. How do I put into words that Mum just wants the best of me? Everything I think of sounds weird. Like, I'm a freak with a freak mother. Everyone thinks it. I hear them whispering when I walk past them in the corridors. They know about my mum and her affairs and the times when she gets fired. This town is small, and people talk.

She wants the best for me. She's my mum. Maybe I should trust Mum when she says that uni won't be any good for me. Maybe she knows what I should and shouldn't be doing.

"Here you are." Mrs Vaughan passes me the leaflet, and I thank her. Then she backs away and goes back to handing out essays. I guess she knows that she's already said enough.

I slip the leaflet into my bag. The school bell rings, so I make my way out of the classroom. The low sun makes me squint as I hurry across the carpark to the bus. It's coming up to Christmas break, and the deadline for university applications will soon be approaching. My estimated grades are good. I could go wherever I want. I could get out of Eddington and find my way in the world. But what if university is like school? What if I don't make any friends, or they call me names behind my back? What if I'm not clever enough, and all my grades have been a fluke so far?

The cold winter air bites my skin as I exit the bus at my stop. Mum won't be in yet. She'll still be at work. What is it now? Another secretary job? Or maybe it's the cleaning job? I can't remember. All I know is that I can eat as many jam sandwiches as I like when she's not around, even if my jeans are getting a little tight. Now that I'm in the 6th form I can wear my own clothes, but the problem is, I don't own anything cool. All my clothes are from charity shops and sales racks. I don't have designer sportswear or the right shoes.

After tucking into my second jam sandwich, I pull the leaflet out of my bag and start to read through it. There are a lot of figures and facts. I'm more of a words person than a numbers person. They make my head spin.

But I keep reading, despite everything. My excitement builds up and up. I see the happy faces of the students on the front of the leaflet and wonder whether that could be me. I could be the smiling girl surrounded by friends. I could work, and learn, and live with people my age, and listen to loud music, and go to concerts. I'd make a best friend and eat ice cream with her while we talk about boys and exams. We'd argue about the washing up or who used the last of the milk, but then we'd open a cheap bottle of wine or go out and drink shots until we passed out on the sofa in a fit of giggles.

I'm so deep into my fantasy that I don't even hear the door open. It's not until Mum is striding into the kitchen that I realise she's home, and I don't have an opportunity to hide the leaflet. I freeze.

"Fuckers. The whole lot of them." She throws her bag onto the table and kicks off her heels. "That fucking little Tracy with her perky tits and big eyelashes. She only has to flutter them at Bob and he's drooling like fat kid in a bakery. What the fuck are you doing? What the *fuck* are you eating?" She snatches the plate away and tosses it onto the kitchen work surface. Our kitchen is so tiny that she only has to turn and stretch her arm. The motion is so fast that she catches me trying to hide the leaflet from her view as she turns back to me. "What's that you've got?"

I place my arm over the pamphlet, ignoring my pattering heart.

"What is it? Why are you hiding it?" she demands.

"It's nothing. School stuff."

"What, are they teaching you about periods? Come on, show me." Her manicured fingers grab my arm and wrench it away. Then she snatches the folds of paper with her other hand. "Financial aid for…" Her eyes move rapidly across the front cover. She lets my arm drop back onto the table, and I rub the sore spot where her long red nails clawed into me. "What is this? You think we're poor? You think we're poor enough that you have to apply for *aid*? After all the work I do for you. Two jobs. Two jobs, Sophie, all to put jam sandwiches in your belly. Fat little bitch."

I stare at my hands as they tremble against the tabletop. I should never have brought the leaflet back. I'm such an idiot.

"Financial aid for university applicants," she reads in a mocking voice. "Miss Smartypants wants to go to university, does she? She wants to be part of the pompous crowd. She wants to leave her mother here to rot on her own because she's a selfish little cow. And after everything I do for you? I work my fingers to the *bone* for you." She shakes her head and backs away from the table, starting to pace back and forth across the length of the room. "I can't believe you'd leave me, at the drop of a *hat*." She snaps her fingers. "To be all alone. You know how lonely I've been since things ended with Mark. And you know it was all your fault. No one wants a moping teenager for a stepdaughter. Why can't you put on make-up and do your hair? Stop shovelling food in your gob for one minute and actually get some exercise. Do you think I look this way from being a slob? I work for it. And if I hadn't had to push you out seventeen years ago, I would look a damn sight better." She runs her hands through her hair. "I'm over the hill now, Sophie. Don't you understand that? I'll never find a man. I'll be alone for the rest of my life, and you're going to *leave* me here to rot while you go off gallivanting with *students*." She starts to cry, great, heaving sobs.

"Mum," I say quietly, holding back my tears. I'm frozen as always, caught by her outburst and too terrified to even move. "I'm sorry I brought the leaflet home. Don't cry." I can't bear it when she cries. The guilt is unbearable. I never meant to make her feel this way.

She wipes her eyes, smearing mascara across her temples. "I just want to protect you, honey. I want to keep you safe because I love you. Don't you know what happens to girls like you who go to university? There are men there. Predators. They wait until you're drunk and put drugs in your drink. Then they take you home and rape you—"

"Mum, stop!"

"It's true! It happened to my friend. Sophie, if you go there, you'll be hurt. I don't want that to happen." She rushes over to me and wraps her arms around me, smothering me against her satin blouse. "I want to keep you safe. You're safe at home with me. If you knew what I've done for you, you'd never question me. You'd never disobey. If you knew what I've given up..."

CHAPTER TWELVE

As the stormy weather fades, the stifling heat returns, turning the children feral and the adults irritable. There are two fights on the playground this week, prompting Moira to call an emergency assembly about bullying and violence. Alisha and I stand on the sidelines as the head talks us through appropriate behaviour and "using our words".

While the atmosphere at school is taut, the atmosphere at home is deadly. Despite a phone call to Erin's superior—and several emails to them both, explaining that there has been a terrible mistake and I don't believe Erin is hurting Mum—she still refuses to come back to work for us. Instead, we have Susanne, an older woman in her late forties who never makes chit-chat and complains about car trouble every time she steps in the door, bringing cigarette breath into our home.

I even try leaving Erin a voicemail to explain

that I believe Mum sent that message during one of her confused moments, but Erin never replies. I don't blame her. I wouldn't want to work in that environment, either. If one of the students ever accused me of something that terrible, I don't think I'd be able to come to school and look people in the eye. So we're stuck with Susanne, a woman whose sour face makes Nurse Ratched seem like Mary Poppins. At the end of each day Mum seems subdued and quiet. I am too. We sit and eat our meals in near silence.

PC Hollis and PC Chowdhury call round to tell me that they have investigated the video and saw nothing helpful, but they will be canvassing the area as well as contacting Peter. They have no proof it was Peter, so it's not like they can arrest him. But they see the action as harassment and make a point of telling me that they take such behaviour seriously. That in itself worries me. Why do they feel the need to reassure me? I can tell they think they have better things to do than follow up on a vandalism case against a bag of clothes meant for a charity shop. They're placating me with their assurances.

I decide not to tell them about my suspicions about Mum. If it is her, it's a private matter.

All day at school I watch the cameras. Susanne is not as bright and breezy as Erin was. She dumps food in front of Mum before sitting down with a magazine. I see Mum flailing her arms, clearly shouting, while Susanne turns away and leaves the room. A few moments later, Mum appears to have forgotten whatever she was mad about, and Susanne returns. I need to take notes from this woman. She doesn't take any of the crap that I've had dished out from Mum.

But most of the time I think about everything that has happened, from the button outside the house, to the time Mum drank bleach, to the voice on the recording and the shredded clothing. Do I honestly believe Mum could be responsible for all those events? Can I imagine her orchestrating each one? Taunting me about the shadow because she knows there's a hidden memory from my past that I can't access? Finding a way to break the camera, logging in to my email and sending that nastygram to Erin's boss? Sneaking out of the house at night? Pretending to lose her keys? Drinking bleach?

The question I cannot answer is whether I believe my mother is capable of all those things. Yes, she can be manipulative and nasty. Yes, she can be cruel when she feels that she's been wronged. But what, apart from existing, have I done to warrant this?

I close the laptop and sigh, which is lost amongst the noise from the classroom. The students are supposed to be reading from *The Hobbit*, but they've taken to chatting and passing notes around instead. I raise my voice and order silence.

There was only Chloe not talking to any friends. My eyes linger on her sat in the corner, gazing out of the window. With all this going on, I forgot to keep an eye on Chloe like I'd said I would. I don't know if she still talks to her imaginary friend.

I'm not on the rota for playground duty at lunchtime, so I stay in the classroom and eat my sandwich. When I check my mobile phone, I see there are a couple of missed calls from a withheld number. Normally I would think nothing of it, but with everything that's going on, the sight causes a chill to run down my spine. It could be Peter again, though his calls seem to have quieted now. I gave his details to the police, and there's a chance they got him to back off. Perhaps this is him returning with gusto, withholding his number so I won't know it's him. I should make a note. Perhaps the police have some way of tracing the call.

My fingers are itching towards the laptop on my desk. If I could just watch some more of the feed, maybe I'll be able to figure all this out. I'm missing an important piece of the puzzle; I know it. I wish I knew what it was.

Chloe is the first child to come back to the classroom. By the way she's holding out her right arm, I can tell she's pretending to hold someone's hand. Her lips are moving, but she's talking so quietly that I can't make out what she's saying. I'm about to call her over so I can talk to her when the rest of the class walks in, and I launch into teaching them about ancient Egypt.

This is a subject I love to teach. I love telling the kids about the mummification process and seeing the expressions of delight and disgust on their faces when they discover that the dead person's brain would be scraped out of their skull. But today it all seems to fall flat. The students are disruptive and mocking, I can't seem to pull my attention away from Chloe, and my delivery falls flat where I usually have an engaged audience. The afternoon is a slog until I split the kids into groups and let them have a go at drawing their own hieroglyphs.

Except for Chloe. I feign a special task for her and bring her to the front of the desk, waiting until the rest of the class are too busy to notice me talking to her individually. I hate to single her out like this, but I feel the need to check on her. And to be honest, I need the distraction from watching the camera feed again. It's becoming an obsession.

"So, how do you like the Egyptians?" I ask, easing into our conversations.

"They worshipped cats," she replies. "That's cool."

"Oh, yeah? Do you have a cat at home?"

She nods. "He's called Fluffy. I named him when he was a kitten."

"Excellent name for a cat. I presume he lives up to his name?"

She grins. "Yeah. Mum goes mad when she has to hoover every day. But it makes him cuddly."

"What does Jessie think about Fluffy? Does she like him too?" I try to mention her imaginary friend as flippantly as I can, as though it's completely normal to act as though Jessie is real.

"Jessie likes Fluffy too." She talks with her head down, concentrating on drawing the hieroglyphs I set her. "But sometimes she gets a bit jealous."

"Why's that?"

"Well, Jessie likes to spend time with me on my own. Sometimes she thinks I spend too much time with Fluffy."

"Does Jessie get upset if you spend time with your friends?"

"I guess." She sounds less sure of herself now.

It hurts my heart to hear that note of uncertainty in her voice. She's at least aware that she doesn't have any friends aside from Jessie. Maybe I can pass that along to Chloe's parents or her therapist.

"Does Jessie allow you to have friends, Chloe?" I ask.

She shrugs. "Yeah."

"What do you and Jessie talk about?"

She lifts her head and smiles. I can tell she feels more comfortable talking about her imaginary friend. "Everything. What we had for lunch. Oh, and we play games too. Like, I hide things and Jessie has to find them. Or we play hide and seek where Jessie has to find me."

The way Chloe talks about her makes Jessie seem so real. Despite my trying to maintain a straight face in front of Chloe, a slight quiver ripples through my stomach. A chill spreads over my skin. I attempt to shake it away. I don't want her to think I believe she's weird or creepy. That won't help her.

Chloe's strangeness isn't the only thing bothering me. When she mentioned playing hide and seek, I heard a distant giggle in my mind. It was so real that I almost turned around to check that one of the other kids hadn't crept up on me. Yet at the same time I was aware that it was a memory. A memory from long ago.

I shake my head and try to focus on Chloe. When I shut my eyes for the briefest of moments, the strongest scent of strawberries ignites my senses. It isn't the smell of fresh strawberries. It's more like the sickly, candied scent of a strawberry lollipop.

"What else can you tell me about Jessie?" I ask.

"She likes the colour purple, Minecraft, and One Direction, but she hates Little Mix and Elsa from *Frozen*. Sometimes she likes to cut my Barbie's hair or paint my nails red. Mum hates that, though."

I nod and smile, trying hard to concentrate. All I can think about is that fleeting moment where things suddenly started to make sense. I force myself to think back. To remember.

There's a garden, and some sunshine. It isn't our garden in Eddington. No, it's harder and dustier. The grass is patchy and yellowed. There's a rusted old bucket in the corner and...

"We make tea together," Chloe says. "We have tea parties in the garden with the teddy bears that Mum says I'm too old for..."

One, two, now you.

One, two, now you.

I'm on my feet. My hands are in my hair, pulling it free from the bun at the back of my head. The room goes quiet. Every child turns to stare at me. Chloe slinks away to the back of the room.

One, two, now you.

I hear the childish voice speaking to me in my mind. Who is that? Is it me?

The memory hits me. It lasts only a few moments, but it's enough to have me rocking back on the heels of my shoes, amazed by the emotional power that resonates within. The pain is like a stab to the gut.

It's a short memory. I'm outside in the garden playing with my imaginary friend, whom I called Shadow. We had a little rhyme: *One, two, now you.* Then one of us would have to do a dare. I'd spoken the words when Mum came into the garden seeming upset and dishevelled. She asked me who I was talking to, and I told her it was my shadow. I remember that she was angry with me for that and told me that I must never, ever play with my shadow again.

The shadow.

I have to get home. Fortunately, the bell rings.

CHAPTER THIRTEEN

Susanne never sticks around for a chat. She's usually waiting by the door with her coat on and a cigarette hanging from her lips, ready to nod her goodbye and go. Most days I miss the cup of tea and a chat I used to have with Erin. But today I'm relieved that Susanne is a woman who wants to leave our house at the earliest opportunity. It leaves me alone with Mum. I have questions for her.

Mum sits on the sofa in front of the television, watching one of those early evening Australian soaps. I'm itching to blurt out the memory. I want to grasp her by the shoulders, shake her, and demand that she tell me what it means. Instead, I think back to my conversation with Chloe. Mum is a little like a child in that her suspicions are easily raised if I appear too eager. I already know that she has been deliberately keeping things from me. I need to be gentle.

I make a big show of getting into my slippers. "Long day today. How have you been, Mum? Are you getting on with Susanne?"

"I prefer the other one," Mum says without even glancing up from the television. "At least that one bothered to make sure my soup is warm."

"I can have a word with her if you like." I have no intention of doing that unless I have to. Susanne is almost as intimidating as Mum, and I've never been able to stand up to her. "How does a nice cup of tea sound?"

"Fine."

"Right, then." I make my way into the kitchen, ignoring a rising, persistent eagerness. My thoughts are impatient and cajoling, trying to speed up time.

"Don't make it weak, like you usually do," she shouts through the wall. "Let it steep, like I told you." Her voice fades into muttering, probably admonishing me for never listening to her instructions properly.

Her voice muffles on as I pace the kitchen, waiting for the kettle to boil. Yet more criticism to add to the pile. I can't even make a cup of tea without her telling me how. That's always been the pattern with us. She criticises me, and I take it. If she tells me my hair is too long, I get a haircut. Then she tells me it's too short and doesn't suit my face. She'll tell me my clothes are old and shabby and I'll never find a man. I buy a new dress, and she says I'm dolled up like a cheap tart. And then there's my jaw, which she never lets me forget.

But of course, I must let the tea steep. I pour the water over the bag and return to pacing the kitchen. Other people wouldn't put up with her. They'd walk out and leave her to her own bitterness. I grew up believing she really did want the best for me, because she'd tell me that over and over. She'd tell me all about how the world was out to get me and how she could stop that happening if I stayed with her. And now here I am, letting her tea steep like the good daughter I am. I take a deep breath and plunge the spoon into the water.

Hold it together, Sophie. I can't get answers if I lose my temper. Thirty-odd years and I've never been able to stand up to her. One of these days I worry I'll crack open. That I'll unleash a monster onto the world. A twisted-up and bitter monster who's sick of it all. But I can't do that today.

A splash of milk. No, a touch more, but not too much. I add extra to mine. I manage to stop myself from slamming the fridge door. Just.

Time to fix that smile on my face. I head back into the living room.

"What are you watching?" I ask, setting the tea down on the coffee table.

"*Neighbours*. It's drivel."

"Turn it off, then," I suggest.

Her eyes narrow. "Is that any way to talk to your mother?" She lifts her tea. I can't help but notice how the action requires more effort from her than it did a few months ago. She blows on the hot liquid. "I gave birth to you, after all. And I never got that twenty-two-inch waist ever again." She takes a sip and shakes her head. "You didn't let it steep. Trust me to end up with the one daughter in the world who can't make a cup of tea."

Next to my legs on the sofa, pressed down into the sofa cushion, I form a fist with my hand so tight that my fingernails dig into my skin. The knuckles on the hand gripping my mug turn white. I take a silent deep breath.

"I was thinking about London the other day," I venture, dipping my toe in to test the temperature.

"What do you want to think about London for? Dirty place. Nasty memories. Like your father fucking the girl from the bakery behind my back."

I flinch. It's a bad sign for Mum to mention Dad. She can easily get off track, wandering down a road of suicide—caused by me, of course; I was such a terrible daughter that I drove him to it—infidelity and crime. But Geoff Howland was a rogue long before I came along. Dad had been arrested for minor offences three times by the time I was born. He never served jail time, but there were some close calls. Apart from his mistakes, I know little to nothing about my father. Someone could show me a photograph of him and I wouldn't know who he was.

"Never marry a man who'll steal for you. Men who steal and lie will cheat as well. Then they'll leave you with an ungrateful daughter who can't make tea."

"Actually, it was a nice memory that I had of London," I continue, hoping the conversation is still salvageable. "I was in our back garden, playing by myself—"

"Well, you didn't have any friends."

"Actually, I think I had one friend." I casually sip my tea. "Do you remember? I used to play with it in the garden."

Mum's back stiffens. She places her tea back on the coffee table and turns back to the television. I can tell that the mood has changed from the way she clutches her hands and the tension of her limbs.

"Though I don't think it was a real friend. It was an imaginary friend," I say. "Don't you remember how I called it my shadow? I think we had a little rhyme that we used to say to each other before we gave each other silly dares: *One, two, now you.* Do you remember the rhyme?"

Anyone would think that she isn't listening to me, but I know better. I see the blood drain from her face and the slight twitch that runs along her jawline.

"I think I will turn this drivel off. And I'm going to pour this down the sink because it's disgusting. Then I'm going to find my keys because I'd left them somewhere but I don't know where. Maybe they're on the kitchen table—"

"Have you been on Facebook today?" I ask. Mum is—or was—a keen Facebook user. She liked sharing cat videos and memes about "putting the

Great back in Great Britain". Before the Alzheimer's she used to play Words with Friends almost every day. "It's great that you're so computer savvy." I sip my tea nonchalantly.

She makes a guttural sound before replying. "That's when I can use the damn thing. These days I forget all my passwords." She laughs, but it doesn't sound real. I'm searching for the lie in everything now. I don't trust her.

"Oh, I think you're still pretty good at it. Hey, weren't we talking about my imaginary friend?" I try to keep my voice bright and breezy despite the growing temptation to yell. "Don't you remember the shadow?"

"Where's my soup, Erin? Isn't it lunchtime?"

"Mum, it's Sophie. Erin used to be your nurse. Remember? We were talking about my imaginary friend."

"I never put up with any of that nonsense," she says. "Imaginary friends are for the strange kids, the ones with the thick glasses who look like they're about to piss their pants at the slightest sound. I wouldn't let my daughter grow up like that."

"But I did have an imaginary friend," I insist. "I remember. The shadow. I remember playing with it in the garden. I think that's why it was so familiar that you kept mentioning a shadow coming to the house."

"I don't know what you're talking about. I never said that, and I never forget what I say."

"You did say it to me, Mum. You said it several times. You said that the shadow came into the garden one night, and then you said it came into your bedroom. Don't you remember asking me to help you check the house for intruders?"

"Would you stop talking, Becca?" Mum gets to her feet and stands with her hands clenched at her sides. She stands so abruptly that the tea mug is knocked from the coffee table and spills onto the carpet.

Yet neither of us rushes to clear the mess. We stare at each other with wide eyes.

"Who's Becca?" I say eventually.

The trance is broken. "You need to clean that up. It'll stain the carpet."

"Not until you answer my question." I'm shaking so much that ripples appear in the tea I'm resting on my knee. "Who is Becca?"

"Some old friend from when I was a child. Back when I had friends. Fine—if you won't do it, I will." She bends down, making a big show of her aching back.

I slam my tea down on the coffee table. "No. I'll do it."

*

After Mum goes to bed, I return to the living room with a large glass of Pinot Grigio. Before I settle onto the sofa, I glance at the reflection in the mirror hanging above the fireplace. That woman is a mess.

Stress, age, and exhaustion have been etched into her skin, like claws dragged across flesh. But that's not everything I see. There's a new spark of determination in her eyes. The slack, vacant expression she used to wear to try to get people to like her is gone, and instead, she frowns. This woman is going to put all the pieces together and figure out what is going on. And she's going to start tonight.

I place my wine on the coffee table and pull two fat photo albums from the shelves above the television. Despite the bulge and weight of the large albums, they seem a meagre offering for a life. They're dusty and unused, spreading dirt onto my shirt. I wipe my hand across the top album as I sit down on the sofa, then shake the dust onto the carpet. Mum would have a fit, but she isn't here right now. She wouldn't approve of the large glass of wine, either. I take a big gulp and lift the glass as if in toast. Then I open the cover of the album.

It's filled with photographs from before I was born. I can't say I'm not disappointed. This one is the thicker of the two, and I was hoping to see more of me as a child. But I remind myself of the mysterious Becca and begin searching through Mum's old photographs to see if I can find pictures of her old friends.

The album begins with black and white photographs of Mum as a child, with her hair in ringlets and her cheeks chubby. I had hoped to see her as a baby, to see if she looked like me, not that I remember what I looked like as a baby. But as a child I see myself in the way she smiles, as though she's unsure. It's strange to see Mum with that expression, because she's always seemed so sure of herself, to the point of arrogance. Could it be that my mum started out life as insecure as the rest of us? I can't quite believe it.

For a little while I get distracted by the photographs of my grandparents. They died when I was too small for me to remember them. These pictures are a fascinating glimpse into a part of Mum's life that I've never seen. We've never been a family to sit around photo albums and reminisce. We're barely even a family. Both of my grandparents were smart people with nice clothes and neat hair. They're attractive, too. Normal. I know there was a big fall-out between Mum and her parents when she married my father. They never approved and, frankly, I don't blame them.

I flip through the pages, paying close attention to any photographs where Mum seems to be with other children, but there aren't many, and someone has been through the album writing dates and names next to the pictures. It can't be my grandmother's writing, because the album doesn't feel old enough. Though I can't imagine her doing so, at one point Mum must have sat down and pasted these photographs into the album, writing diligently next to each picture.

There are no Beccas. Not even a Rebecca or a Becky. I move on to the next album.

It begins with my parents' wedding picture. The first thing I realise is how young they both were. Mum was only twenty when I was born, but I was in her belly when this photograph was taken. She isn't showing yet. I'm the size of a bean, sat waiting in her womb. Waiting to be born.

I push the album away for a moment, choked by a sudden urge to burst into tears. Another gulp of wine and a deep breath and I pull the album back. I need to hold it together if I'm going to get anywhere.

After the wedding picture, there are a couple of my parents with Mum wearing early eighties maternity wear. The photographs are hazy and often barely in focus. The two of them are laughing and joking around. Dad always seems to have a drink or a cigarette in his hand. They are sometimes with other people, but there is no writing in this album, so I can't find anyone called Becca.

And then the album stops.

I skip through blank pages with my heard thudding against my chest. There used to be photographs here, but they've all been pulled out. I can see the lines of glue with patches of torn paper still stuck to them. I skip forward at least twenty pages until I find a picture of me.

I pause. With trembling fingers I reach out and touch the photograph of me. I'm alone, perhaps six or seven years old, and I'm dressed in my school uniform. My hair is in a long plait, and I have a wonky fringe that I remember Mum cutting for me: *Hold still or I'll slap your bare bottom*. I'm smiling that same smile I saw Mum smiling as a child, unsure, hesitant and anxious.

I flip the page. There's another photograph of me. This time I'm ten or eleven, and I'm holding a trophy. Mum stands next to me. I remember what the trophy was for. I won a prize for a science project about volcanoes at a school fete. I remember one of the teachers suggesting that she take a picture of the event, and Mum reluctantly letting her.

The next page is a photograph of me, Mum, and one of her boyfriends. Bob? Bill? Frank? They all had names like that. They were usually married, so I don't expect to see many more photographs of them. Sure enough, the rest of the album is a mishmash of awkward photographs of me on a rare day out to Blackpool, or taking part in some sort of school event, or Mum drinking wine and smoking with the girlfriends she used to fall out with every week. There is the occasional boyfriend, nearly always bald and burned from holidays in Spain or the sun bed. There aren't any photographs of me after the age of about fifteen.

We barely celebrated birthdays when I was growing up, and we never had a big dinner on Christmas day. I suppose it hasn't really hit me— not until this moment—how strange that was. But what stands out the most are the missing photographs, which would have happened right around the time I was born. There are no baby photographs of me at all. There's nothing until I'm at least six. Where have they gone?

CHAPTER FOURTEEN

I'm searching, but I don't know what I'm searching for. Yes I do: evidence. I need to see it for myself. I need to see my mother faking the extent of her illness and doing these things to hurt me. I need the proof. At school, I can't wait to open my laptop and plug in my headphones so I can listen to the file from that night. I listen to it while I watch Mum over the camera feed. I listen to that voice over and over, imagining her leaning towards the recording device and hissing out that rasp to fool me.

You will know me.

Maybe that's what it means, her final reveal. I get to see the true vileness of her nature. I get to know who she really is. What's her secret? Betrayal? Murder? All kinds of dark thoughts flit through my mind when I think about the missing photographs, the shredded clothes, the voice in the night.

At night, I take my laptop to bed with me and keep a bottle of wine on my bedside table. I watch the cameras and sip my wine and almost will my mother to act suspiciously. One night she actually does get out of bed. I get so excited I spill Chardonnay all over the bed sheets. It turns out she's going to the toilet. But the interruption in her sleep causes confusion, and I find her asleep on the landing. I have to wake her up and take her back to bed. At first she doesn't know who I am.

At least, that's how she acts.

Back in my classroom, I put my head on my hands and rub my tired eyes. What am I thinking? She's had tests and scans. There's no doubt that Mum has Alzheimer's. But there is a chance that she's making it seem worse than it is, pretending that the disease is progressing faster while she's actually still relatively lucid. All to drive me insane before the dementia washes her clean.

The bell rings, and the students filter out for lunch. It's only at that point that I realise I haven't set them any work for the last twenty minutes. I've been sat at the front of the classroom, staring at my computer screen, while the children talked amongst themselves. I watch Chloe follow the rest of the students out of the classroom and don't even have the energy to worry about her anymore.

When the door opens and Moira walks in, I quickly shut down my laptop and smile, hoping it doesn't appear too fake.

"Good lesson?" she asks. "It sounded pretty

boisterous in here."

"Oh, yes, it was a great lesson today," I lie. "Everyone was having a lot of fun. We were acting out scenes from *Romeo and Juliet*." I hope my bright red face isn't an obvious indication of my inability to tell a convincing lie.

"Good, good." Moira's sensible heels click against the classroom floor as she walks towards the first row of desks. I usually straighten up the classroom while the kids are at lunch, but I haven't bothered today. Chairs and desks are askew. I watch her trace a finger over the backrest of a chair with a pattering heart and a dry throat.

She pulls one of the chairs away from the front row and drags it towards my desk. She sits on the chair and leans over my desk, giving me a pitying smile followed by a sympathetic head tilt.

"How's your mum doing?"

I feel like this is going somewhere. In fact, I know it. I pull at the sleeves of my top, nervously searching to give my hands a task. "The disease is progressing more quickly than I'd hoped. And we've had some problems with the nurses. We recently had to switch to a different nurse, which has been a difficult transition for her." I fail to mention that there's a possibility I'm being stalked by my own mother.

"And what about you? Are you okay? Are you coping?" The head tilt moves to a more severe angle, and her smile appears to freeze.

Irritation creeps up my skin, prickling at my

nerves and making me grit my teeth. "I'm fine."

She straightens her neck at last. "Are you sure, Sophie? I want you to be completely honest with me, because this is important."

"Honestly, I'm fine. I'm tired, of course, and I'm stressed. But I'm still on time every day. I know I missed a couple of days, but term is almost over and I can catch up on sleep and get myself sorted out for next term."

"Good. That's good. Because, well, quite honestly, we've had some complaints from the other members of staff. And a couple of parents."

My jaw drops. "What?"

"Your class has been a bit disruptive recently. You're making a lot of noise. And you've missed playground duty a couple of times. Also, some of the students haven't had their homework back for a few weeks, and their projects have gone unmarked."

"I... I know I'm a little behind, but..." There's no end to that sentence. She's right. I have let things slip. It's not the students' fault that my personal life is falling apart or that I'm a mess inside. "I had no idea it had got this far."

"Sophie, you seem exhausted. I hate to point it out, but you do look a mess. We're all worried about you because we care about you. Okay? If you want to take the rest of the term off for stress, we can find a substitute teacher to fill in for a couple of weeks. That way you'll have a long rest during the summer break and you can come back right as rain for next year. How does that sound?"

"I... I don't..."

"Why don't you have a think about it today and meet me tomorrow lunchtime for a chat? I've already got an agency on hold in case this is what you'd like to do." The chair scrapes across the linoleum as she stands. "We want what's best for you. I hope you know how valued you are."

But as she leaves the classroom, all I can think is that the words sound empty.

*

To top off my day, a withheld number calls my mobile phone repeatedly until I turn it off altogether. As it happens, I've never been watching the camera feed when the phone rings. It's always been at times when I'm driving or have my phone in my bag, so I can't say for sure it isn't Mum at least some of the time. It could also be Peter, or anyone else for that matter.

At the end of the day I find myself stalling. I take my time rearranging the classroom. I mark a couple of maths questions from the test I set the students this afternoon. I glance at my sparse lesson plan for tomorrow, which I should have fleshed out but haven't bothered with. And then Alisha walks in.

"Hey, Soph." She wrings her hands together and stands awkwardly a few feet away from me. That's not like Alisha. She's a hugger. She's someone who has no clue about personal boundaries. That was one of the things I liked about her, the fact that she would always be close to me, always liberal with little touches and kisses on the cheek. After a lifetime of coldness, her warmth was refreshing.

But not today. All that warmth has gone, leaving us with a huge gap where our friendship used to be.

"Did you know the head was going to have a little 'chat' with me?" I ask, not bothering to keep the venom from my voice. "Were you one of the staff members who complained about the noise coming from my classroom?"

"No. No, I didn't complain, but I did say that I was worried about you—"

"What?"

"Hear me out, okay? You've not been talking to me much recently. In fact, you've barely spoken to anyone. You're always cooped up in this classroom, staring at whatever is on that damn laptop. I thought we were friends, but you're shutting me out of everything. I want to help you." She takes a step forward, holding out her hands. The pleading expression on her face makes me turn away.

"Then find a way to support me, because every time we talk, all you do is try to make me dump my mother into a nursing home." As I say the words, I realise they have become an instinctive defensive reaction and nothing more. I've changed so much over the last few months that I no longer desire to help Mum. No. That's not why I want to keep her at home. It's because I want *answers* from my mother. I want the truth. But Alisha doesn't know any of that, and I can't tell her. If I tell anyone, they might think I'm even crazier than they do right now.

"Sophie, I'm sorry I... Oh, Sophie. Don't cry."

But I've finally cracked, and I don't know how to patch myself back up. I fold into Alisha's arms and sob on her shoulder, letting at least some of it out while holding a little back because I worry that if I let it all out, I'll never stop crying.

"We're broken," I whisper as the sobs finally begin to calm. "We're both so broken, and I don't know how to fix it."

"I'd do anything to make you realise that you can't keep this woman in your life. Anything," Alisha says.

*

I turn down an offer of a cup of tea and head to my car, even though the tea is more than tempting. I want nothing more than to sit with my friend and chat. I want to talk until my jaw is tired. I want to offload everything that's pressing me down. But I can't. This weight is for me to carry alone, and I can't shed it until I've found out that last piece of my past. It's only Mum who can provide that, but I have to get it out of her gently before she shuts everything down forever. Sometimes I wonder who is hunting whom. There are times when I feel like an animal stuck in a trap—and there are other times when I feel like a hunter stalking a dangerous wild animal, treading softly through the forest.

"You're late." Susanne speaks with her lips moving around the cigarette dangling down. She lights the fag as she bustles out of the door.

I'm almost sad to see her go, because while she's here I don't have to be alone with Mum.

"I can't stand that woman." Mum appears in the doorway between the hall and the living room as I'm taking my shoes off. "She smells like an ashtray."

"You used to smoke," I remind her. "I thought you wouldn't mind the smell."

"Well, I do. What happened to the other one, the one with the piercings? I didn't like her much either, but at least she didn't smell as bad."

"We upset her," I reply, without going into much detail.

"Young girls scare too easily these days. We're made of tougher stuff." Her gaze travels up and down my body. "Well, I am, anyway. You look terrible, by the way."

I pass her in the doorway and head into the kitchen to pour a glass of water. "That's because I have you to look after and a job to hold down."

"Oh, I'm a burden, am I? Why don't you throw me in a home, then? Condemn me to death, like I know you want to." Her eyes sparkle. She's found something to fight against, and that's what she loves more than anything. "Just let me die and have done with it."

I lean against the kitchen table, digging my fingernails into the wood. The heat spreading over my skin is daring me to let it all out, to scream at her, tell her what she's done to me over the years, to accuse her of driving me mad as she plays on her illness as cruelly as she can. I want it more than anything. My fingernails dig harder until the tips of my fingers are in pain.

We stand there, squaring off. Two women with irreparable damage spreading out like a canyon between us. She stands with her shoulders wide, arrogant, almost daring me to fight back, like she has my entire life. The only difference is that her sardonic smile—the one that spreads across her face when she realises I'm too chickenshit to stand up to her—never comes. There's only a wariness about her. I'm not acting as beaten-down and pathetic as usual, and that frightens her.

When the phone rings, we both start. But for me, it unleashes a molten pot of boiling rage. All I can think about are the missed calls and the constant texts from Peter. I'm sick of being bothered.

I snatch up the receiver and bark down the phone. "Leave me alone!"

Only instead of the heavy breathing that I've come to expect, a meek female voice replies, "Is that Sophie Howland? I'm so sorry to bother you. My name is Eileen Woods. I'm Peter's mother. I think we need to talk."

CHAPTER FIFTEEN

Eileen is the kind of woman you expect to find in a library stamping books. She has a meek mouse appearance, complete with thick-lensed glasses and short greying hair set in loose curls around her face. She waves to me as I enter the café. When I frown in confusion, she explains that Peter showed her my profile picture from the dating website.

"I know my son is a complicated man." She fidgets in her chair, as though the words make her uncomfortable. "I'm sorry if he's been bothering you. He tends to latch on to people. But you should know that he's harmless."

I keep stirring my tea to waste nervous energy. "Are you sure about that? Someone broke into my house. I left a bag of clothes on my step for a charity, and someone cut them to shreds."

Eileen leans back, her eyes wide with shock.

"That doesn't sound like Peter at all. He's never done anything like that."

"That you know of," I point out.

"Yes, that's true." She breaks a cookie in half and stares at it. "He's always been an odd duck. I know people are always afraid of loners. I tell myself that my Peter wouldn't be one of those men who end up on the news, that he would never hurt a fly. But that's what they all say, don't they? The mothers."

"Why did you want to meet me?" I ask.

"I try to reach out to anyone Peter might have latched on to. I want them to know that he has someone in his life who is here helping him. He's loved." She smiles, and the warmth is genuine. For a brief moment I actually believe that this woman could prevent her troubled son from hurting anyone.

"He's not violent," she insists. "All he's ever done is call the women he tried to date. He calls them a lot for a while, and soon enough he gets bored."

"And moves on to the next one." I lift an eyebrow to illustrate how odd his behaviour is.

"I've tried to stop him going on these dates," she says. "But he gets so lonely."

"I'm sorry, but I think your son needs help. He needs to speak to a professional."

"Oh, he has, in the past. He's a little autistic, you see. He can hold down a job okay, but none of his relationships have ever worked out."

I cringe at the thought of this lonely man growing old without a companion. Of course I feel sorry for him, but I'm afraid, too, of what that can do to a person. What happens when Eileen dies and he's left completely alone?

"Have any of these women had a restraining order taken out against him?"

She sighs. "Yes. One. It was a few years ago, and I must say that he's much better now. But at the time, he started following this woman. You see, things progressed further with her than anyone else." Eileen's lips pursed. "She was what I'd call a loose woman. Poor Peter thought he was in love this time. He kept turning up at her house long after the woman had broken off the relationship. But he was nearly physical with her."

"Did he ever vandalise her property?" I ask.

"No, never." She shakes her head firmly.

"Look, for what it's worth, I don't think Peter is the one who cut up my clothes. I think something else is going on there. But he has been calling me a lot, and if you could get him to stop... It's just that I'm under a lot of stress at the moment." Embarrassingly, my voice cracks.

"Oh, you poor love." Eileen delves into her handbag and produces a packet of tissues. "After your coffee, Peter mentioned that you had a sick mother to care for. I wasn't sure if it was true, or..."

"It's true," I reply. "She has early onset dementia. It has taken quite a toll, and with these phone calls and everything else..."

Eileen leans forward and squeezes my arm. "Say no more. Don't you worry about my son. I'll take care of it."

On the way home, I can't help wondering what my life would have been like if I'd had a mother like Eileen. Someone to pass me tissues when I was upset, to call me "love" and make me cups of tea.

I head back home to quickly pick up some extra marking before school starts. Eileen had agreed to meet me at 7:30, before we were both due at work. But as I pull up the car, Susanne is storming out of the house yanking a cigarette from her packet.

"She's tapped, that one," she calls out.

With the front door wide open, Mum stumbles out onto the drive in her bare feet.

"Don't you ever come back, you whore. I know you stole him from me."

I'm not sure what to address first, so I turn to Susanne. "What's happened? You know she gets confused. She has Alzheimer's."

"Yeah, that I can deal with," Susanne replies as she attempts to light her cigarette. "But punching me in the face? Throwing her cup of tea at me? Look at this bruise! How the old bird has the strength, I don't know. This is a hostile working environment. Your mother needs two people around at all times. I need to go home."

I sigh, completely deflated at this next turn of events. I can't argue with Susanne, not when the shadow of a bruise shines along her left cheekbone.

"All right, you go. I'm sorry that she hit you.

She's not been in her right mind."

"That's the thing," Susanne says. "She wasn't even confused at the time. She was plain old mad at me for getting her tea wrong. That woman was a cruel, stone-hearted bitch long before the Alzheimer's."

I open my mouth to defend her. That's what I do. I defend Mum's behaviour. I've done it my entire life. But not anymore. I've changed. The part of me that has been chained to her my entire life is now free.

There is no way to defend her, so I shut my mouth and let Susanne go.

"Come on, Mum. It's just you and me now."

*

After getting her settled, I pick up the phone and call the school, requesting that they put me through to the head teacher.

Moira's voice is as clipped and no-nonsense as always when she replies. But I detect a slight tone of pity as she uses a higher register and speaks more slowly than usual. "Sophie. Is everything all right?"

"That offer for sick leave—is it still on?"

"Of course," she replies.

"I'd like to take it. And I'd like it to start today."

I tell her about the nurse, about Mum's assault, and how I have to stay with her all day now. She's calm, patient, and kind with me, traits that I've never expected from her. When I disconnect the call, I know I should be relieved, but I'm not. Aside from the sadness, I feel cheated, as though a gift has been snatched from my fingers. All my life I've felt uncomfortable in my own skin, as though I'm not truly who I say I am. That's the real reason why people avoid me, and why most of my friendships and relationships have fizzled out. I think Jamie saw that in me but was attracted to it. Attracted to my insecurity.

But being at the school gave me an identity. I was Miss Howland. I was well-liked and respected by my students. I'm a good teacher, confident in what I do but not unpleasant about it. Now that's gone—at least for now—leaving me feeling like a lost teenager with no direction in life.

"I've wet myself."

I turn around to find Mum standing in the kitchen holding her crotch. The air is filled with the tang of urine. Mum's bare feet are in the centre of a puddle of pee, her skin covered in the urine.

"That's all right. It's only a little accident. Let's get you cleaned up."

I help her up the stairs. She's frailer than ever before, and tears wet her nose. I pity her. But most of all, I wonder if this woman, this bent over, piss-stained person, could also be the same person who's been stalking me and driving me crazy. She drank bleach a few weeks ago. She forgets my name and forgets the name of her nurses. She wet herself and needs help getting into the bath. How can this be the same person sneaking around the house cutting up my clothes and hacking into my email account?

I bundle up the soiled clothes and put them straight into the washing machine while Mum soaks in the bath. Then I clean the pee from the floor and disinfect everything she touched. Then I help Mum back out of the bath, dry her off and help her into a nightgown. All the while, she calls me Mummy.

This will be the only time I hear that word. Uttered by my own mother. Yet, even in this dark moment, they make my stomach ache for a little girl to say them to me.

After I get Mum back into her bed, I slip downstairs, run the taps to fill the sink, and cry until my eyes are sore.

I want that ache to go away. I want, more than anything—more than I want to know the dark secret in my past—to feel whole. Because I never have felt whole. I've always felt as though a part of me is missing.

When the breakfast pots are cleared away, I take a glass of water up to Mum.

She sits upright in bed when I see her. For once, there's a bright smile on her face. I set the glass down on the bedside table and watch as she opens the top drawer and takes out a bottle of pills.

"Look, Sophie—I'm taking them all at once, like you told me to," she says.

I watch as she opens the pill bottle and takes one

out. She slips it into her mouth and swallows it down with the water. Then she takes another pill from the bottle and opens her mouth to take it.

I snap out of my trance. "No! Mum, no. Don't take that. I never told you to take all the pills at once. Don't ever do that."

With shaking hands, I remove the bottle of pills from her fingers and leave the room.

CHAPTER SIXTEEN

My laughter echoes. Every time I laugh, I hear it sung back to me, like a bird imitating the human voice. That laughter makes me feel lighter. It's a young laugh. A child's laugh. I'm a child.

There's a hand in mine, pulling me forward.

"Come on, Shadow."

I trot along, faster. I'm running. It's the end of summer, and I'm thinking about ice cream—the kind with the flake and strawberry sauce—but I'm also sad. I feel forgotten.

Then the sky goes dark, and I'm running faster. The hand that was in mine has gone, and there's a dull pain in my chest. I cry out, but there's no echo for my cry. I glance down at my body expecting, somehow, to be pulled in two. Ripped in half.

I get the sudden, real feeling that I'm being chased, and I glance behind me to see the silhouette of a man following me. The moon outlines him, revealing his bulk. I urge my legs to carry me faster, tripping over the ridges in the pavement. Though it's dark, I know where I'm going.

My hands ball into fists as I run. I lift my right hand, and the moonlight shimmers across the strands of hair in my fist. The pain in my chest grows tighter and tighter, until tears run down my cheeks.

"Mummy?" I say to no one.

The man is gaining on me. I know he's going to catch me up.

I stare at the hair in my hand as I fall, and I know that I will never be the same again, because I've lost who I am.

*

I wake with a gasp, tangled in bed sheets. My hands fly up to my face to find my skin hot with a fever and damp with sweat. A smattering of fine hair falls over my face, and I realise that I've pulled out my hair in my sleep again. Touching the back of my head confirms it. There's a light coating of blood on my fingertips.

The clock says 6:15. I don't need to get up for work today, though I do need to make breakfast for Mum, and since I've enforced this early morning routine, she'll be expecting that soon. But first, I wait until my heart is back to a normal rhythm, and until the shadowy figure from my dream has gone when I close my eyes.

Every image in my dream evokes a vague sense of memory. That feeling of déjà vu spreads over my skin like cold custard. The significance of all the pieces is clear, but I can't put them together to give me the answers to all my questions.

Come on, Shadow.

Was that someone talking to me? The way I remembered the existence of the shadow made me believe that it was someone, or some*thing* else. Nothing makes sense. Maybe this hair-pulling thing is a tic, or a habit from when I was little. The secret that my mum is keeping from me—could it be that I was disturbed as a child? That I'm mentally ill?

I repress a shudder at the thought. I block it from my mind. None of it explains the man chasing me in my dream, or the familiar streets and the little-girl giggle that I heard. My mind swims with all the disjointed images as they fragment and fade away. I want to dash into the living room and write them on the notepad I keep next to the phone, but I'm afraid that if I move, I'll forget everything. So I stare down at the hair in my hand until I've committed as much as I can to memory. Then I swing my legs over the side of the bed and get up. On my way out of the room, I drop the strands of hair onto my dressing table.

Mum is still sleeping when I pop my head around the door, which surprises me. I decide there's no point in waking her up, seeing as there won't be a nurse coming this morning. And I don't have a job to go to, which means I can spend as much time in the shower as I like. I suppose there is an upside to taking leave.

The luxurious heat of the shower brings my body to life, though the abrasion at the back of my head smarts when I shampoo my hair. If I carry on with these nightmares, I'll end up bald. Perhaps I should mention this to my doctor, seeing as I have to go to get a sick note to sign me off for stress at work. That shouldn't be too hard, thanks to my worrying colleagues. If everyone else believes I'm stressed, then I suppose I must be.

I can't help letting bitterness creep in. It's followed by that familiar punch in the gut as I grieve over my lost job. Will I ever go back? Will they ever want me again?

My mind drifts back to the nightmare. That same dull ache strikes my chest. I remember gazing down at my body and expecting to be ripped in two. Deep down in my bones, I know that is important—as vital as the awareness of my own brokenness. There must be a cause for all this internal anguish, and it must be connected to my childhood. My maturity is twisted up with the way Mum brought me up, and I can't untangle myself.

Mum is still sleeping half an hour later as I get dressed and dry my hair. Perhaps I still can get a moment to myself, even when I'm caring for her full-time this summer. Maybe we'll manage to bond together, fixing whatever it is that's been broken between us before the disease takes her away forever. Or maybe that's wishful thinking.

I tie my hair back to disguise the growing bald patch and head downstairs to make breakfast. While the kettle is boiling, I boot up my laptop and check on the camera in Mum's room. It seems fine. Nothing has been altered this time. I rewind a little and watch her sleeping for a while. Then I close the laptop lid. Perhaps everything has blown over, and whatever Mum might have been trying to do has now ended. I make my cup of tea, think about my nightmares and my strange almost-memories, and wonder how much of all of this has been in my mind.

I used to be a positive, optimistic person who always looked on the bright side. But over these last few months, I've lost that characteristic. I've lost a lot. If only I can make a new start, perhaps I can learn to find that missing part that I've been searching for all my life.

It's a beautiful morning outside, and the sound of birds singing filters into the house. I move across to the glass doors of the kitchen that open out onto the garden with the intention of taking my tea and toast to the patio table.

I never make it to the patio table. I don't even get to open the French doors leading out into the garden. My wrist goes limp, and the hot tea splashes up my shins. At my feet, the mug shatters into tiny pieces. Even with the pain of the hot liquid against my legs, I find myself transfixed and immobile. A small cry escapes my lips.

There, on the glass doors, is a clear handprint. Someone has been in my garden. They have walked up to the glass doors, they've placed their hand on the glass, and they've stared into my home.

*

PC Hollis and PC Chowdhury arrive promptly at nine. By that time, I've distracted myself from the handprint by getting Mum out of bed, dressing her and making her breakfast. I explain to her that two men are coming round to the house to ask me a few questions but that she doesn't need to be there. She can take her jigsaw puzzle into the living room. For once, she complies without question, and I'm glad.

The two officers examine the handprint, take some photographs and check for shoeprints in the garden.

"Has anything been taken from the garden or the shed?" PC Chowdhury asks.

"I checked earlier," I reply. "Nothing has gone."

"Did they break into the house?"

"No. At least, I don't think so. It's just the handprint. Isn't that trespassing, though?" I ask.

Hollis nods. "Trespassing is a civil matter rather than a criminal one. But with the other incidents that have occurred here recently, you can be assured that we will take this seriously. You're being harassed, Ms. Howland."

I let out a sigh of relief. "I'm glad. I half-thought

that you might just ignore it."

"No, no. There will be an investigation. You mentioned that you have a security camera at the back of the house?"

"Yes. I've not watched the footage yet. It probably sounds silly, but I didn't want to watch it alone," I say.

"That's perfectly understandable." Hollis smiles.

I load up the security system on my laptop, pulling up the feed from last night. I rewind the footage until Hollis tells me to stop and click play. He has a good eye. He caught the movement before I spotted it.

I let the video play. The three of us crowd around the laptop, each engrossed in the images on the screen. My heart patters against my ribs as I watch the events of last night unfold. As the footage plays, I'm aware of the blood draining from my face and the nausea that rises from my belly. Hollis gives me a quick, worried glance and a half-smile. It helps, but it doesn't stop the dizziness. I grasp hold of the kitchen chair, desperately needing the extra strength.

It's a dark, moonless night, and at first the camera doesn't pick any movement. But then, when a car passes along the street that runs parallel with our garden, its headlights illuminate a figure standing at the very end of the lawn. I have to clamp my hand against my mouth to stop myself from crying out when I see it.

The figure is more of a person-shaped lump

than anything else. I can tell that the person is short, that they're wearing a long, dark-coloured overcoat, that their face is angled low, and that they're wearing a hat. The overcoat is bulky, hiding their shape.

It's a fleeting, terrifying glimpse. Then the car continues down the road and the video goes dark once more. My eyes are still transfixed on the spot where the person was standing.

When our outside light is triggered, I do let out a sound akin to a whimper. This time I fail to hold it in. It prompts PC Hollis to turn and ask if I'm all right. I nod and continue watching the recording.

The figure is now close to our kitchen, and the outside light shines brightly on our trespasser. They stand with their feet planted wide, with gloved hands at their sides and their face angled down so that their features are hidden. If I once felt that I could explain all this away by blaming local kids, I now have confirmation that I cannot. There is calculated determination behind all this. I see it in the way they stand, the way they wait... It all suggests that they're aware of the camera, and they know exactly what they're doing.

When the figure steps closer to the door, I think we all three experience the sensation of a spell being broken. We all start at the sudden movement. Even Chowdhury lets out a soft, nervous laugh. Without lifting his or her head, the trespasser slowly starts to remove the glove from their left hand. My heart skips a beat as I watch them lean forward, obscuring their hand from the camera. They lean forward and press their hand against the glass, covering the action with their body.

When the deed is done, they scuttle away quickly, turning fast and keeping their head angled down the entire time. I let out a long, bittersweet sigh of relief.

"Whoever it was knew about your security camera," Hollis says with a frown. "Can we take a copy of the footage from last night?"

"Of course. Do you think you'll be able to see anything more?"

"Well, we can't enhance the images any further. It's not like TV crime shows, I'm afraid," he says with a grin. "But we might pick up on any little extras that might help. We should be able to determine the height of the suspect."

"They seemed about my height," I reply.

He nods. "I thought that too."

"Peter was short," I mumble.

"We spoke to Peter Woods after the incident with your clothes. I'm afraid there was little more we could do other than warn him about the phone calls," Hollis says. "But we had no evidence that he was the vandal then. Perhaps we'll find more evidence after this incident. The phone calls alone could be enough to get a restraining order, if that's what you'd like to do."

Chowdhury takes notes and nods at his partner.

"His mother called me the other day, and I met up with her for a coffee. I think she was concerned that Peter had, in her words, latched on to me. She said that he does this a lot with women. He fixates on anyone he goes on a date with and calls and texts them until they get fed up of him."

"We'll talk to him again," PC Chowdhury says.

"If there's anything you need, Ms. Howland," PC Hollis says as they head out of the house, "don't hesitate to call. Try not to worry. There's no indication that this person wants to harm you. But to be on the safe side, keep your windows and doors locked at night. And take care."

Perhaps it's because he appears to be showing me that he cares, or perhaps it's because he's a policeman and seems like a protector, but I can't help feeling suddenly insecure under his gaze, like I want to put on lipstick or redo my hair. It's an odd sensation and one I haven't experienced since meeting Jamie.

I thank the two of them and close the door behind them, then lock it with the key and the bolt.

I pour a glass of water and nip into the living room to check on Mum. She's sat on the sofa with her jigsaw puzzle laid out on a tray on her knee. But instead of focusing on the puzzle, she's staring out of the window at the cars passing by. I decide to leave her to it.

When I'm back in the kitchen, I boot up the laptop and check the footage from the other cameras in the house from last night. Before the police arrived, I'd briefly viewed the video from Mum's room, but I hadn't paid much attention.

My appetite finally hits, so I settle onto one of our kitchen chairs with a sandwich and begin watching. Mum goes to bed at the time I remember. She's asleep almost immediately.

She's a contented sleeper who barely moves. I watch and watch, occasionally skipping forward. Every so often, she rolls over and clutches the duvet. Then she's still again for a while. I shake my head. This is ridiculous. Do I honestly believe Mum is the person in the garden?

I'm about to give up when I see her roll over and clutch the duvet again. It's almost identical to the last time she did it. I rewind and watch it again. Then I rewind back to the last time she moved. It *is* identical. The video is a loop of the same hour over and over again. There are no headlights streaming in through the light fabric curtains. There are no changes in the shadows in the room. This entire night is a fabrication.

And if the footage from Mum's room is a lie, that means I can't trust anything I see on the cameras.

"Sophie."

I stand so abruptly that the chair tips up behind me. "What is it, Mum?" My voice is shaking as I call back to her.

"Come here a minute," she shouts.

I close the laptop lid and make my way through to the living room. As I step foot inside the same room as my mother, I'm sick with anticipation. She must know about the cameras. She knows I'm watching her. I don't know how she did it, but she outwitted me yet again. What is she going to do next?

"Come closer, Sophie," she says.

"What is it, Mum?" Despite trying to sound confident, I sound the opposite. Squeaking my words like a frightened mouse.

"Do you see that?" she asks, pointing towards the window.

I follow the direction of her finger. There's a smudge on the window. Forgetting my concerns, I'm lost to intrigue. I turn my back on Mum and step towards the glass.

She's right. There is something there. It's a word, written by a finger, and written very small.

Shadow, it says.

CHAPTER SEVENTEEN

I've taken to carrying the locks of hair in my pocket, and whenever I sit and watch the camera feed, I twirl the hair around my fingers. It's comforting.

I don't trust anything the cameras record anymore. Instead, I sit at the kitchen table while Mum works on her jigsaw puzzle in the next room, and I watch the live feed. I take the laptop to bed with me and place it on the bed next to me, drinking wine while I watch Mum sleep, checking for patterns, checking that she hasn't somehow replaced the live feed with a recording.

Mum is pretty good at navigating the internet, but is she capable of recording herself sleeping, creating a loop, and uploading it onto the computer? I spent a few hours discussing this very issue with the helpdesk for the security system I bought, and they spoke so much jargon it made my head spin.

The problem with my mother is that you can *never* rule her out. When I found myself rejected from every university I applied to, I thought I wasn't good enough. It wasn't until much later, when I bumped into Mrs. Vaughan, that she told me how surprised she was to see that I'd been rejected. I was a good student, she said, which was why she'd never understood the poor personal statement I had submitted along with my grades. She even went as far as to dig my application out of the files to show me. It was not the statement I'd written. It was drivel, filled with grammatical errors, typos, and a long paragraph about my desire to come to university for the parties. By that time, I'd completed my teacher training and had started at Eddington. If I'd discovered Mum's betrayal in my teens, I might have finally been persuaded to leave her and live my own life. I remember the huge row I had with Jamie when I confessed that I knew what she'd done. He couldn't believe that I'd never confronted her. But I couldn't see the point. The past was the past. Nothing could change that.

Now I know that I was wrong. The past always catches up with you; at least, that's what I'm banking on.

It's eleven in the morning and I'm already eying the opened bottle of wine in the fridge when I retrieve milk for my cup of tea. Since I've been caring for Mum full-time, I've ordered a large delivery of groceries from Tesco and stocked up the house. Shopping with Mum is a complete nightmare. Last time, she wandered off in the freezer aisle and shoplifted a Mars bar. I didn't realise until we got home. It didn't seem worth it to take her back, so I let her eat the Mars bar.

Instead of reaching for the wine, I take out the remains of a chocolate fudge cake I started eating at midnight and shovel a large slice into my mouth. As I'm licking the creamy filling from my fingers, the doorbell rings.

"Who is it?" Mum barks.

"How should I know?" I reply. I wonder whether it's the police calling round to tell me more about the trespasser. The fingerprints have now been washed away, along with that chilling word. *Shadow*.

The police took the fingerprints, of course, but I haven't heard back. PC Hollis warned me that there would only be a slim chance that they'd find our trespasser on "the system".

My fingers are still partially covered in cake crumbs and frosting as I open the door to find Peter standing on the front step. My first instinct is to try to slam the door shut, but he's too fast. When I swing the door, he jams his foot in the way with those big boots of his. Then he has a hand on the door, pushing it towards me.

"Please, Sophie. I just want to talk." His eyes are wide and beseeching, but also slightly deranged.

I cringe away from his dirty skin and hair. The

man smells like he hasn't showered for days. "If you force your way into the house, I'll call the police. Mum! Mum, get the phone."

"All right." He backs away, raising his hands to placate me. "But please listen to me for a few seconds. Please."

I slip the chain on the lock and angle my head so I can see him through the gap. "Make it quick."

He shakes his head and his shoulders sag, reminding me of the "before" footage of a rescue dog. "I... I don't understand how you could do that to me. Don't you know what you did to my head? You've messed me up! How could you lead me on like that and then never call me back? Did you do it to hurt me? Is that it? Did you want to break my heart? I love you, Sophie. What we had was special."

"It was a coffee, Peter," I say. "Look, I'm going to call your mum, okay? I should call the police, but I won't this one time if you leave now and never contact me ever again."

"How can you be so cruel? After everything... How could you make love to me and then treat me this way?"

He takes a step towards the house, and I back away.

"What did you say?" I whisper.

"How could you make love to me and then never speak to me again? It was such a beautiful night. I know you had a good time too."

The sight of him, the smell of him, and those

words—those cloying, terrifying words—make my stomach lurch. The chocolate cake is dangerously close to hitting the hallway carpet. How can he believe these things? I can see it in his eyes. He actually believes that we've had sex.

"Peter, listen to me really carefully. We have never, ever had sexual intercourse. We haven't even kissed. It was one coffee—"

"You look different." He takes another step closer to the door, and I cringe away from him, hiding behind the chain. "Your hair, or… something."

The stress eating has resulted in some quick weight gain, and the drinking has made my eyes puffy. That must be what he's noticing. Jesus, I must appear even worse than I realised.

"I'm closing the door now, and I want you to leave. But we never had any kind of sexual relations. I think you must be confused."

As I close, lock, and bolt the door, I can hear Peter insisting otherwise. I hurry through the corridor into the living room.

"Who have you been screwing?" Mum says with a sardonic smile on her face.

"Why didn't you bring me the phone when I asked? Can't you see the man is insane? I haven't been *screwing* anyone. I've been stuck here taking care of you."

Mum's face contorts into a twisted expression of hatred. "You're not the daughter I wanted. You're all *wrong*."

Half in the act of searching for my mobile phone, I turn and stare at her. She blinks, and her eyes go out of focus. Then she begins moving the jigsaw puzzle pieces around on the tray on her lap. I redirect my gaze to the rest of the room and find my phone on the armrest of the sofa. I'll have time to worry about yet another of Mum's strange outbursts later.

As I make my way back into the kitchen, I scroll through my contacts until I find Eileen, Peter's mother. The camera at the front of the house shows that Peter has finally left. Even thinking about him makes my skin crawl. I push away the last crumbs of my chocolate cake and try to keep my breakfast down.

Eileen answers with a bright hello.

"Your son has gone too far."

"Who is this?" Still chipper, like an early morning news reader.

"It's Sophie Howland. Your son has been to my house claiming all kinds of lies."

"Oh, dear."

"It's a bit more serious than that," I say. "He has fabricated some sort of relationship between the two of us. I haven't called the police yet, but I'm going to have to."

"Please don't—"

"This has gone too far. They need to speak to him about the stalker who's been at my house anyway. I think it's him, and you need to stop enabling him."

"But he wouldn't hurt anyone—"

She's crying when I hang up, and I'm shaking. Whether that's out of fear or anger or even pity, I'm not sure. I take a deep breath and call PC Hollis.

He listens patiently as I tell him everything that has happened, even though the more I say, the crazier it sounds. What if he thinks *I'm* the one making everything up? What if he believes I slept with Peter and treated him like shit, or I was the one who cut up my clothes? At least I couldn't fake the handprint on the window or the figure coming towards the house. Unless he believes I snuck out there and did it. No, he took my and Mum's fingerprints. They can rule us out as suspects.

I'm relieved when he assures me that I was right to worry and that they will be questioning Peter as soon as possible.

"Ms. Howland, though I do believe your case is extremely important and I will prioritise this, you should know that we're particularly stretched at this moment in time. I obviously can't go into details, but you should be aware that it may take us a few days longer to work through your case."

The little bit of hope that I allowed myself to hold on to begins to fizzle out like a deflated balloon. "That's okay. I know you're doing everything you can."

"There's no indication that Peter will do anything to hurt you," he continues. "Carry on with what you're doing with the log. Notify us if he gets in contact, and keep your doors and windows locked. We can talk further about a restraining order in due course."

I hang up the phone not feeling any better than when I called.

*

I keep the windows and doors locked, but it starts to feel more like I'm locking myself in with Mum than that I'm locking the doors to keep people out. I find myself with a constant need to check my mobile phone for missed calls, but there are none. Eileen doesn't call back.

As I make lunch for Mum and tidy the kitchen, I work through a deluge of disparate thoughts. Peter's words and his deranged eyes keep going round and round in my mind. And then Mum's comment: that I'm *wrong*. What if there is something wrong with me? What if all of this is in my mind?

I can't eat, only watch the cameras. The neighbour's cat almost gives me the fright of my life when it jumps over the wall into the garden. I don't even have the energy to bang on the window when it starts to do its business in the flower bed.

Mum shuffles back to her sofa while I finally open that bottle of wine. After the first glass, I pop my head around the door.

"Everything okay?" I can't help but notice that she has hardly progressed on her jigsaw from this morning. But her problem-solving skills are diminishing by the day.

"Yes, Becca," she says. "I'm fine working on my puzzle."

"Sophie."

"No, dear. Becca." She smiles as though I'm the stupid one.

Maybe there's more to this Becca person than she's letting on. Talking to Mum is becoming increasingly like banging my head against the wall, and I didn't find anything about a Becca when I went through the photo albums. But there might be another option. With my laptop under one arm and my glass of wine in the other hand, I make my way upstairs to Mum's room.

Crossing the threshold with the intention of snooping is both exhilarating and terrifying. When I was growing up, I was never allowed in Mum's room. Since she's been ill, I've been in and out of her room to care for her, and, of course, I planted the camera to check up on her. But I've never properly searched through her belongings. I've always been too afraid to do anything like that.

Mum is a lot neater now than she used to be. I occasionally dust and hoover in here, but Mum keeps things tidy. She always puts her own clothes away, and her drawers are always firmly closed. In the weeks of watching the cameras, I haven't seen her do anything strange in this room. She doesn't drag anything out from under the bed at night or act suspiciously. But I have a vague memory from a few months ago. I came into the room to wake her up and found her sat on the blanket box at the end of her bed, staring at what I thought was a photograph. But when she realised I was there, she quickly hid the photograph in the pocket of her dressing gown. I never mentioned it to her because I didn't want to embarrass her. It was clear to me that I'd intruded on an intimate moment, and I didn't want to press. It felt too alien to have anything even resembling a heart-to-heart with my mother.

I head straight for the blanket box. This is where I saw her with the photograph. This is where I start. When I lift it gently, the lid opens with a slight creak. The smell that greets me is like talcum powder and dust. I've never been in this box before, so I didn't know what to expect, but I thought it was where Mum keeps spare bedding and blankets. I was wrong.

It's more of a keepsake box. There are a few old rusting biscuit tins and a locked box. I lift one of the tins out and flip open the lid. It's filled with letters. With a jolt, I realise they are unsent letters to her mother, my grandmother. Every single one is dated. I read the top letter:

January 20th 1990

It's all your fault. If you hadn't been such a terrible mother, if you hadn't forced me away, I would never have had to do this. I would never have had to make that decision. I hate you with every ion in my being. You were a hateful, spiteful hag, and I hope you rot in hell with Daddy.

I would have been ten years old. Five years after we moved to Eddington, so five years after Mum spoke to my grandmother for the last time. I always thought that Mum had gone to Grandma to borrow money for our move, but from this unsent letter, it would seem unlikely unless Mum was able to hide her true feelings when she asked for the money. Mum can be manipulative when she wants to be, but I've never known her hide her anger. Her temper is too all-encompassing for that. It boils over, and God help anyone who gets in its way. Her temper has a personality all by itself.

My fingers are trembling as I flick through the rest of the letters. They are all filled with the same vitriol. Some are addressed to Grandma; others are addressed to my father. None of them goes into any detail about what it is Mum had to do, but they all mention an "unforgiveable" event. It's the top letter that has been opened and read the most. The pages are thin and crumpled, with yellowing stains along the edges. This is the one Mum opens and reads the most. I close the tin and place it back in the box.

I'm surprised to find an old woollen jumper of mine in the box. With a jolt, I remember finding the same jumper in the attic a few weeks ago. When did Mum go up into the attic and retrieve it? The feel and the smell of the thing bring memories rushing back to me. Mum was obsessed with this being my favourite jumper, but I hated the thing. I remember being about six years old, when it was already too small for me. She insisted that it was my favourite, but it always made me itch and I hated the smell. The smell made me sad. I lift the jumper to my face and inhale.

The punch to my gut is instantaneous. There it is again: that dull ache, as though I'm grieving a life I never had. Maybe I'll always feel this way when I lift a piece of children's clothing. Maybe I'll always get this tearing feeling running through my body, as though I'm going to be pulled in half by the pain. How is it possible? How is the strength of this emotion so intense for an experience that I've never even had?

When I hear the steps coming up the stairs, the child in me takes over. I hurriedly stuff everything back in the box and am hurrying out of the room when I see Mum at the top of the stairs.

"What are you doing?" she asks.

"Just some dusting."

Her eyes narrow for a moment, and I think she's about to comment on the fact that I don't have a duster. "That cat is in the garden again."

"Oh, ignore it," I say.

"All right. But it's dead."

WALES, JUNE, 2014

The clouds hang low in the sky, like dark, deflated balloons. Our car is surrounded by long stretches of fields that fall away into the distant sea. I'm wearing a waterproof jacket, waiting for the rain. Jamie checks the weather app on his phone for the third time in the last five minutes.

"We should never have chosen Pembrokeshire in June," he says. "The only guaranteed weather for this time of year is abroad."

"Mum won't fly," I reply. "Besides, I wanted to come here. I've never been before. The countryside is beautiful. Don't you think?"

"It's no different to Yorkshire, if you ask me." His words are forced between his gritted teeth. He pushes his smartphone back into his jeans pocket and folds his arms. "They should be here by now. The adverts say that they always arrive within the hour. Lying bastards. This whole thing is just a fucking disaster. Why did we even bother? And why the hell did you let your mother put diesel into the car?"

I roll my eyes for the third or fourth time in the last ten minutes. My patience is wearing as Jamie's temper rises. "Stop going on about it, for God's sake. You were in the bathroom, and she agreed to do it while I nipped across the road to get a coffee. I thought she knew what she was doing. She's had cars before."

"She knew exactly what she was doing," Jamie mutters.

"Don't be ridiculous. Why would she want the car to break down? Who would want to be stuck waiting for the AA when it's about to piss it down?" I gesture angrily towards the gathering clouds.

When Jamie moves closer, a tiny speck of spit flies from his mouth and lands on my cheek. "Why do you think? Because she didn't want to come in the first place. Because she hates me and wants to undermine me. Because she's a vindictive bitch. Take your pick."

"Would you keep your voice down? She's only a few feet away." I brush away the spit and pull my jacket tighter, trying not to look at Mum, sat nice and warm inside the car. "You can't say these things about my mother. It's not right. I know she's difficult, but I need you both to get along."

Jamie lets out a hollow laugh devoid of all good humour. "Difficult? Impossible, more like."

"You have to try."

I can't decide whether I'm cold from the cool breeze coming off the sea, or Jamie's frosty glare. Mum and Jamie have been at war since the moment they met. Mum has a way of winding him up, and Jamie doesn't have any patience with her at all. So far, there have been tense, almost painful meals that ended up with either or both storming off, silent evenings in front of the TV punctuated with bitter remarks, and moments when the constant complaining from each of them about the other person got too much for me.

"I don't know what else I can do. I try to be nice to her, and she calls me weak. I stand up to her, and I'm aggressive. She find fault with everything I do. And, quite frankly, Sophie, I'm sick of standing by and letting her find fault with everything you do. She has no respect for either of us, and I'm starting to think she has no respect for anyone at all. You're better off moving out."

When I fail to respond, Jamie's light blue eyes penetrate mine. I open my mouth to speak, but nothing comes out.

Jamie's shoulders slump. "You'd be happier with me. We can settle down and start a family. I thought that was what you wanted?"

"It is, but—"

"But what?"

"I can't just leave her."

"Sophie, that's what children do. They grow up, and they live their own lives. You're still a child. At least you act like one. It's pathetic."

The wind slaps me in the face along with his words. The rain finally starts to fall, but neither of us moves. Inside the car, Mum sits with her head against the glass. Napping.

"You know you'd have a better life with me," Jamie continues. His skin shines from the rain. His blond hair is plastered to his forehead. He's looking older. I never noticed that before. He's a few years older than I am, but he has a baby face. This is the first time I've looked at him and seen him at his true age. "I can give you what you want, but I won't do it with her in my life. I can't raise children with her around."

"What?"

"You heard me. She's toxic. I won't have that influence on my children."

"But—"

"It's time to make a decision, Sophie. You can't live a happy life with that woman in your life. It's either her or me."

"I can't believe this. I can't believe you're saying these things."

The rain begins to run down my neck. It bounces off the hood of the car and splatters onto the road. I can't believe that Jamie is putting me in this position, and I can't believe that Mum would sabotage our holiday just to spite us. Am I stupid? Am I hiding with my head in the sand, hoping that everything will be okay? Am I the loneliest woman in the world right now?

The AA van pulls up.

CHAPTER EIGHTEEN

The kitchen doors are wide open when I hurry downstairs. Mum has already been outside. Why didn't I hear her? How did she find the keys that I hid?

She points the cat out to me, not that she needed to. I can hardly look at the twisted thing. My breath is frozen in my throat. I gesture for Mum to get inside, then I lock the doors.

"How long were you outside for?" I ask.

"A few minutes."

"How did you unlock the doors?"

"With my key, how else?" She turns away and whispers, "Fucking moron."

I start to ask her how she found them, then change my mind. I need to call PC Hollis.

I get his answering machine and leave a message. When I hang up, my fingers linger over the 9 key, but I can't bring myself to call the emergency services about a dead cat. Without Hollis or Chowdhury—who know what has been happening to me—I don't feel confident that anything will happen. I take a few photographs on my phone through the kitchen door. Another sinister entry for my log.

I dread the next phone call. The number is in my contacts after a disastrous week-long holiday with me, Mum and Jamie in Wales. I'd asked Mrs. Hamilton from next door to water the garden for us. In the end we'd hardly needed to bother. We abandoned the holiday after two days of constant rowing between Mum and Jamie.

I punch the number into my phone and hold my breath. When it comes to trying to explain what happened, I'm lost for words. Instead, I wimp out and tell her that her cat is lying in our back garden and appears unwell, and that I would have come to the house but Mum and I have a sickness bug and I don't want to pass it on. She's welcome to come and get the cat. Then I herd Mum into the living room and shut the kitchen door so I don't have to see Mrs. Hamilton's reaction to finding her cat.

My throat is choked and my hands are shaking. I wish I'd had the foresight to bring the bottle of wine with me. Luckily, I did bring my laptop, which I open and frantically check through the camera feeds.

They're all blank.

How can that be?

"You're always on that thing," Mum notes. "Found yourself another fancy man, have you?"

"Shut up," I snap.

Her teeth clamp together with an audible crack. "You'll be glad when I'm dead, won't you?"

"Just shut up," I repeat. "I've had enough of you."

"I'm not going to sit here and be spoken to like this." She gets on her feet and heads towards the kitchen door.

"Fine. Go upstairs to your room, but do *not* go outside. Where are your keys?"

"What?" Perfectly on cue, her face slackens.

If it's an act, it's a bloody good one.

"Give me your keys."

"I don't know what you mean."

I put the laptop down and move towards her. There must be some new determination in the way I hold myself, because for the first time ever, Mum actually appears afraid of me. She backs up against the wall and holds her hands up.

"I'm not going to hurt you," I say. "I just want your keys." I delve into her trouser pocket and retrieve the keys. They're the spare set that I had hidden in the kitchen table drawer. Mum must have noticed and taken them. "Nothing gets past you, does it? How sick are you really, Mum? How much of this is all an act? Are you messing with me? Are you trying to make me as crazy as you are?"

The slap almost knocks me sideways. My face

burns from the sting of her hand against my cheek. Tears spring into my eyes. Bent low and vulnerable, I glance up to see her hard, remorseless face glaring down at me.

"Have some respect for your mother," she says. And then she leaves the room.

*

I stand in the living room clutching my hurt cheek, wondering how I'll recollect the last few weeks. Will I think of my crazy mother? My crazy stalker? Or my crazy self? Because I'm beginning to wonder if my mind is conjuring half the things that are happening to me. What if I *did* sleep with Peter but can't remember doing it?

What if I brought all this on myself? It was me who got fired at school, and it was me who installed those stupid cameras that have done little for my piece of mind, and a lot for turning me into a paranoid obsessive. I don't even know how Mrs. Hamilton's cat died. It could have had a tumour or a cat stroke or something.

It could have been Mum. It could have been Peter.

I snatch my mobile phone from the coffee table and decide to make one more phone call.

I almost stop dialling the numbers before I complete the call, but I steel myself and continue. I don't know what it will achieve, but I need do *something*, and it might just make me feel a little bit better.

"Hello?"

"Your son is sick."

"Sophie?"

"I found a dead cat in my garden."

There's an intake of breath, followed by a pause. "He wouldn't do it. He's not like that."

"It's time to take your head out of the sand and wake up," I say.

Her voice hardens. "Did you see him kill the cat?"

"No, but—"

"Have you got any proof whatsoever?"

"No—"

"I'm sorry for what you're going through, but quite frankly, you seem a little unhinged, and you did have sex with my son without calling him." I attempt to interject, but she continues. "You're a whore, and you got what you deserve. Now leave me alone. Oh, and Peter's a vegetarian. He would never hurt an animal."

When she disconnects the call, I realise I'm laughing. This has all become far too ridiculous.

The cat is gone, I see when I peer out the window. I pull a fresh bottle of wine from the fridge and take it through to the living room. I wonder if Mum is reading her spiteful letters while she's upstairs. I pour a large glass of wine and take a couple of headache pills to numb the pain.

I can stop this. I know I can. But it means doing the one thing that I don't have the strength to do.

Thinking about it makes me nauseated.

I have to stand up to my mother. I have to demand that she tell me what the hell has been going on. Forget Peter. He's a complication in my life, but he isn't the root of the problem. I just keep hoping that he is. No, the real issue is whatever Mum did all those years ago that meant we had to leave London. How did she get the money to buy a house here?

I drain the glass of wine and pour another one. When I load the laptop up, the cameras are still blank. With everything that has been going on this afternoon, I forgot to call the helpline and tell them that their extremely expensive CCTV system has been a bag of shit. In my drunken haze, I wonder whether I can get a refund, and then laugh at the mundane thoughts swimming through my mind along with thoughts of "Who is my stalker?" and "Is my mother trying to drive me insane?"

My body comes loose from the alcohol and painkillers. After draining another glass of wine, I lie down on the sofa, just to rest my head for a moment, trying to quell the anxiety-ridden thoughts. They dissipate as I slip into unconsciousness.

One, two, now you... It's the last thing I hear as I drift away. That sickly-sweet, high-pitched voice. My mind is all jumbled up. It was *me* who spoke those words to my imaginary friend. Yet, in the midst of my shattered thoughts, it seems as though they are being spoken *to* me.

It's all wrong. *I'm* wrong. Mum said so herself. My *shadow* is my imaginary friend.

Come on, Shadow.

In my dreams, I'm running along the same street as in my nightmare with the man chasing me. I pull my jacket closer to my body against a slight chill in the air. The tall trees dotted along the pavement are beginning to turn golden from the start of autumn. I'm alone. I get the vague feeling that I shouldn't be alone, that I was with someone and now they've been taken away. I can still smell their strawberry lollipop, and my hand stings from where they were gripping me tight.

The sun sets slowly, drowning the sky in ink. Fat tears roll down my face, and my stomach is heavy with dread. There are thoughts swimming through my mind.

How am I going to tell her about the bad man?

She won't understand. She'll blame me.

It's all my fault.

I slow down to a walk, suddenly not wanting to go home. For the first time, I examine the space around me, and then I realise that I'm not where I thought I was. My chest tightens when I understand that I've run past the street that takes me home. I've been running for so long that I've entered another neighbourhood.

There's someone walking up ahead. A woman pushing a pram.

She bends down to me. "Are you lost?"

I nod.

She grabs me by the shoulders and shakes me. *Shake. Shake. Shake.*

Her mouth contorts into an angry grimace. "You need to wake up. Wake up and remember everything."

When I sit up on the sofa, I can't breathe. I pull in three long breaths, surprised at how cold the air is. Surprised, too, by the loud wailing of a house alarm. My heart thumps away, knocking hard on my ribs. *Bang. Bang. Bang.* I run my fingers through my damp hair and catch my breath, groaning at the pain and terror left over from my dream. *Bang. Bang.*

It isn't just my heart. I spring up from the sofa, knocking a half-empty glass of wine onto the carpet. It doesn't take me long to find the cause of the banging. The front door is wide open. The house alarm is from *our* house.

"Mum?" I shout up the stairs.

There's no answer. I hurry up to her room to find the bed empty and my mother missing.

CHAPTER NINETEEN

I don't know how long I slept, but it's the darkest dark when I hurry out of the house. The security light must be as broken as the cameras. It's in almost pitch black that I stumble down the pathway towards the road. Finally, as I make my way past the hedge by the pavement, I find myself illuminated by the puddle of light from the streetlight.

Intoxicated and groggy, I run clumsily into the road shouting Mum's name. My hair is wild, spilling across my face. Strands fly across my eyes as they're caught by the breeze. I slow down for a moment, trying to shake the hair from out of my gaze.

The air around me changes. At first it seems to be a change in atmosphere, as though the very atoms of the air have altered. Then, I notice the scent. Perfume. Peppery and sharp, but unmistakably perfume. I gasp. A body whispers against mine. Panicked, I spin towards the movement. I freeze when I see the dark figure dash past me. With my mouth agape, I stare after the figure, which melts into the darkness as though it had been conjured from my mind. The wind lifts my hair as I stand motionless in the middle of the road, searching for the mysterious figure.

"Mum!" I cry out.

The very marrow of my bones is ice. I shiver as I stare at the street; all I see is the long road from my dream, with the leaves that are turning golden and the smell of a strawberry lollipop. I'm a child again, a small, frightened child. I wanted Mum back then, but I was afraid to tell her what had happened.

That's when it hits me. The dream isn't a nightmare—it's real. It's a memory.

Back in London all those years ago, I ran down that street with the trees and the golden leaves and I was afraid someone was chasing me. I was also afraid of going home because I thought Mum would be angry with me. I was in pain, but I don't think I was injured. I felt the pain deep down, like an ache in my stomach. The same kind of ache that I got when I lifted the jumper out of Mum's blanket box. The same pain I wake up in every time I have that dream.

I wish I could remember why I was running down that street, and why I was in pain.

"Sophie?"

The voice pulls me back from my thoughts. I

hurry across the road to number seventy-six on the street, owned by an elderly lady. She stands in front of the open door, letting the light from her house spill into the street.

"Sophie, she's here. I was on my way to get you."

I let out a deep breath and jog over to the door. "Oh, thank you. I'm so sorry. She must have found my keys and wandered off." I rack my brain for her name. Agatha? No, Agnes.

"She's in the kitchen drinking a glass of water. Come on in."

Agnes has a tiny frame made even tinier by the oversized dressing gown drowning her body. Despite being in her eighties, she moves with ease as she directs me into her home.

"Maureen, your daughter is here."

Mum sits at the kitchen table, ignoring Agnes's Chihuahua yapping at her heels. She doesn't seem to notice me as I step through the door.

Agnes turns to me. "Would you like a cup of tea?"

"I couldn't. It's late, and we've already woken you. I'm so sorry to have put you out like this."

"Sophie, love, I'm eighty-two. I don't sleep much these days, anyway. In fact, most nights I wake up and end up doing my ironing." She chuckles. "Have you been okay recently? I don't want to sound like one of those nosy neighbours, but you don't seem yourself, and that little nurse hasn't been round as much."

"Thank you for asking." I clear my throat, hoping that the wobble in my voice wasn't noticeable. "We're fine, really. Things have been difficult recently. Mum hasn't been herself. I should get her home and to bed. Thanks again for everything you've done. Mum, come on. It's time to go home."

But Mum sucks through her teeth to make a *tsk* sound. "You were always the bad one, Becca. Why can't you be more like Sophie?"

"I am Sophie, Mum." I smile at Agnes to try to ease the tension. She glances away, trying to give us space, but before that I spot a glint of pity in her eyes.

"You're not Sophie," Mum says.

Reaching the end of my patience, I take hold of Mum's arm, more roughly than I intended to, and pull her up from the chair. Without saying anything more, I lead my mother out of Agnes's house and back to ours.

The door is still wide open, and the echo of the shadowy figure seems to fill the entire house. I bolt the door behind me. I think we both feel, in that silence, that the essence of the house has changed irrevocably. I know, deep down, that once I remember it all, we can never go back to how things were. We regard each other and the silent house. This is it.

LONDON, NOVEMBER, 1985

This isn't our garden. It's colder here. The grass is soft and spongy under my shoes. I'm waiting for Mum to come back. She's been in this strange house for a long time.

I'm glad my shadow decided to come along too. I like having the shadow around. It makes me feel better, and I don't hurt as much as I used to. The only thing I don't like about the shadow is that it never talks back. I want it to more than anything, but it won't.

One, two, now you.

Silence.

Oh, well. I suppose I should do it myself.

"I dare you to hold a slug for two seconds. Okay, Sophie, here goes." I lift the fat, slimy body and place it on my palm. "One, two, now you." I pass the slug towards my shadow, but it doesn't hold out its hand. "I'll be brave for both of us, then. One, two. Now it's four." I throw the slug back onto the grass and shake my hand. "Yuk!"

There's the sound of a door opening behind me.

"Mummy!" I call. "I'm playing dares with my shadow, like I used to with—"

"Stop that." She strides over towards me in the way I don't like. "There's no shadow. Stop doing this." Her face is red and angry when she leans over and presses it towards mine. I shrink away, wishing I was the slug right now. I want to cry, but I won't. That only makes her shout more.

"I've sorted it," she says. "We're leaving."

"Are we going home now? I'm cold. I like the slugs and my shadow, but I don't like the cold here."

"We're leaving home as well. We're going someplace new." She takes hold of my arm and pulls me towards the gate.

"Will it be warmer there?"

She shrugs. "I don't know. You'll have to wait and see."

"Is Becca coming with us?"

Mum stops dead. Her face pales and her fingers tighten around my arms. "Becca is dead."

I don't like it when she says that. It makes me want to cry.

"Don't ever talk about Becca again." Her eyes are so hard that I'm more afraid of her than ever before.

I don't want to stop talking about Becca. But maybe if I do, Mummy will like me again.

CHAPTER TWENTY

It's the first time I've remembered anything from that far back in a long time. It popped into my mind as I was warming milk on the stove. I glance over at Mum sitting quietly at the table. She has her jigsaw puzzle in front of her again. I moved it from the sofa for her to work on with more space, but she hasn't made much progress over the last few days. Her eyes are unfocussed as she holds a piece between her fingers.

She will always be the same mother I saw in my memory, at least to me. She will always evoke a certain amount of guilt and fear from me. I can never erase the screaming, the manipulation, and the psychological cruelty that I now recognise for what it is, but she is changing slowly into a child with her illness, and I don't know which version of her is worse.

"Are you hungry?" I ask.

She doesn't answer. I pour the milk into a mug and retrieve a pack of chocolate digestive biscuits from the cupboard. I take both to the table and sit down opposite her.

"Mum, I made you warm milk. Let it cool for a few minutes, okay?"

She nods, but I'm not convinced that she registered what I said.

I slam my hand down on the table. "Are you doing all this to drive me insane?" I blurt out. "Is it all you? Is this an act? Did you send that email to Erin? Did you cut up my clothes and drink the bleach on purpose?"

She stares at me again. Her eyes are slowly coming back into focus. Her expression changes from fear to confusion and then slight defiance. That's when I know she's coming back from the fogginess of her Alzheimer's.

"Mum, who is Becca?" I ask.

"I don't know." She squares her jaw and folds her arms.

"You've called me Becca three or four times now. You can't keep pretending that you don't know who she is. She's someone from your past, isn't she?"

"Becca is dead." She turns away, still with her arms folded across her chest.

"Okay, that's progress. But why do you keep calling me Becca? You know my name. I'm your daughter. I'm Sophie."

"Sophie is dead."

I let out a groan in frustration. "No, I am not. I'm right here. I'm Sophie! Look at me, Mum. Tell me what you're playing at. Is this all to punish me? Haven't I lived up to whatever ridiculous standard you set for me? Did I frighten away your many boyfriends with my mere existence? Am I too ugly to be your daughter?"

"Stop it! Stop saying these things."

"Then tell me who Becca is!"

For the first time in a very long time, Mum's eyes fill with tears. I've seen her cry before, but it's usually in the midst of a guilt trip, when she's claiming that I want her dead, or I want to leave her. I've never seen her cry like this—quietly and reluctantly—as though she's trying hard not to open a part of her she's had locked up for years.

"I can't tell you."

She's not going to tell me, at least not like this. I get up from the kitchen table, leaving her to the unfinished jigsaw, and make my way up to her room. Then I open the blanket box at the end of the bed and begin my search.

"What are you doing? That's private. Those are my private things."

Mum has followed me up to her room. When she sees that I'm searching through her things, she rushes to stop me. Her fingernails scratch against my arms as she tries to claw me away from the box. I push her aside and continue pulling letters, old documents and biscuit tins out of the box. I open the tins and throw the contents onto the carpet, spreading them out as Mum tries to snatch some of the papers away. She kneels on the floor opposite me, snarling and shouting. But I am a different woman now. I am a woman who needs answers, who is determined to understand what is happening to her—and what happened to her in the past. I will not be bullied. I will not be deterred. I am the immovable object that my mother has never encountered before in her life.

"What's in this locked box?" I ask, holding it up.

This box provokes an even stronger reaction from her. She flies towards me. Batting away her hand, I throw the box onto the floor with as much force as I can. The flimsy old lock springs open, spilling photographs onto the carpet. Mum lets out a high-pitched noise from her throat and frantically searches through the contents. She snatches up as many of the pictures as she can, but it's too late. I've seen them.

I've seen the two children that feature in every single one.

I lift a photo from the floor, and a wave of emotion passes over me. My throat closes with the unspoken scream clogged there.

Now I know.

Now I remember.

SARAH A. DENZIL

LONDON, SEPTEMBER, 1985

It's not too far home. We can walk there in ten minutes. I'm sure of it. At least, I keep telling myself that.

Today, at school, Mrs. Ellis got us mixed up again. But that's okay; everyone gets us mixed up. Sometimes I feel like *I* get mixed up, too. I get called Sophie *and* Becca all the time.

There's only one person who never gets us mixed up. She always knows who I am. That's Mum.

Mum forgot to pick us up from school today, but it's okay. We can walk home.

We managed to sneak out before the teachers held us back. We don't like waiting in the classroom with the teachers. We know that it gets Mummy in trouble. She's probably still at work or with Simon, her new boyfriend, who she says is definitely not our new daddy. I keep asking when we're going to get a proper new daddy, but she

214

says that if we hadn't driven the other one to his death, we wouldn't need a new daddy. I suppose she's right.

It's colder today. I think Mum forgot to put our warm coats on this morning. She forgot to pack our Penguin biscuits, too. And my sandwich didn't have butter on. I think Mum is still sad about Dad. She keeps forgetting lots of things. Sometimes she forgets to wake us up for school. Sometimes she forgets to pay the bills as well. There was a man who came to the house and took our television. Mum threw her slippers at him, but he still took the TV, and now we can't watch *Coronation Street*.

Even though it's a bit cold, it's still quite sunny, and the leaves are going golden. I like it when they fall from the trees and you can throw them at people. My legs are tired, but we only have the park and then the street home.

"Does it look dark?" I whisper.

But she doesn't hear. She's leading me, like she always does. She says that I'm her shadow. That makes me feel good and bad. I like being close to her, but I don't know if I always want to follow her. When we're together, it feels like we're one person. *SophieBeccaSophieBecca*. It's good-bad. Maybe I need to be alone sometimes.

"Hey, cutie pies."

She stops before I do. She turns around first. I would have kept walking, but she stops.

"Who are you?" she asks. She's always the one who talks first. That's one of the reasons why I get so confused when people mix us up. She's always the one who talks first.

"I'm a friend of your mum's. She said she was running late and I was to come pick you up. Look, I brought lollipops. They're strawberry. Your favourite."

The man is tall and wide and his eyes are like dirty pebbles. I've never seen him before, and I don't believe he is Mum's friend, but I can tell Becca wants the lollipop because she's pulling me towards him…

CHAPTER TWENTY-ONE

That was the last time I saw my twin sister Becca. The man snatched her, and I tugged and tugged at her hand. When I lost her hand, I tried to grasp her hair, but he pulled her away, shoving his grubby hand over her mouth. I stood there and I watched him run away with her in his arms. The strawberry lollipop fell onto the grass. I carried her hair in my fist all the way home and told Mum what had happened.

"I was her shadow," I say. The photograph in my hand is of the two of us, arms entwined, sat on the sofa like it was any other day. "I followed her around. She was always the leader."

"What do you remember?" Mum asks.

"I remember the park. I remember running home in tears. I remember the weeks afterwards with the police tramping through our house with their big boots. I remember crying myself to sleep

SARAH A. DENZIL

every night. I remember that after she was
snatched, I started talking to my own shadow,
because it was the closest thing I had to her. Why
did I forget all of this?"

"Because you were so young. It was probably so
painful."

"Is that why we moved? To get away from the
memories?" I ask.

"Yes."

"Is she... is she dead?" I ask.

"I don't know."

The room is silent. I begin picking up other
photographs of the two of us together. Here are our
baby pictures. Here are our toddler photographs.
Here we are with Dad. Here we are as a family.

I begin speaking in a hoarse whisper, the words
that have been etched on my bones since I was a
little girl but have remained unspoken all this time.
"I always felt like half a person. I have been
missing a part of me since she was snatched from
my hand in the park. I blamed myself. I have
carried the guilt for a crime I could not remember
all these years."

Mum says nothing, but she reaches across and
picks up the jumper I found when I searched the
box the first time. She rubs the material across her
face, and I shudder at the memory of the itchy
fabric.

And then I shoot up onto my feet.

"What is it?" Mum gazes up at me with wide,
open eyes.

"You... you made me wear that jumper. You said it was my favourite. But it wasn't. I hated it."

Mum shrugs. "So, I got mixed up."

I shake my head. "No, no, you didn't."

Because it's all starting to make sense. "You made me wear that jumper, and you used to say to me, 'Becca is gone. Becca is never coming back.'"

"Because she was taken."

"No," I say. "That's not it. When I found you with Mrs Hamilton earlier, you said to me that I was always the bad one, and you asked me why I couldn't be more like Sophie. Then you called me Becca."

"Sophie..." Her face pales. In the dim light of her bedroom, she is a ghoul. A ghoul that has taken the form of my mother. Or maybe a mother in the form of a ghoul.

"It wasn't Becca who was taken." The words taste sour. I take a step towards her, balling my hands into fists. "You dressed me as her. You called me her name."

"I... I didn't..."

"Yes, you did. You always knew which of us was which. Daddy got mixed up sometimes. The teachers at school were hopeless. But even when we tried to play tricks on you, you always knew. I could never fake her confidence, and that's why you always knew her."

The truth is so horrifying that I don't want to say it. I'm not sure I can utter the words.

"I'm not Sophie. I'm Becca. They took your

favourite, and you've been trying to make me her all these years. But I've never lived up to your expectations, have I? Because Sophie was the confident one. She was the leader. I was the shadow because I always followed her. If Sophie had stayed with you, she would have been your match. She would have talked back, rebelled, stood up for herself, and you would have respected that. But I never did. I sought your approval at every turn, and you never respected me. You've treated me like a doormat all these years because *I let you*."

When I stop speaking, my body trembles. My knees are weak, but I continue to stand. I want her to look up at me for once in her life.

"You've always been a victim," she says. "You can't blame me for that. At every point in your life you've made the decision to be a victim. To be a martyr. You could have left years ago, but you never did. You chose to stay here. You chose Jamie as your only boyfriend. You whine about everything, but you have no one to blame but yourself. And do you know what? I blame you too. I blame you for everything. But most of all, I blame you for Sophie, because they were supposed to take *you*."

The room narrows and blurs. When I blink, I see the hatred in her eyes. I see her true face. Then my knees collapse and I sink to the floor. "What?"

"Nothing. I've said too much. Put these photographs back in the box. *Now*."

I grasp hold of her wrist as she tries to scoop up

the pictures from the carpet.

"In the letter to Grandma, you mention doing something unspeakable. Unforgiveable..."

"Get off me, Becca." She swings her other arm towards me, but I catch her.

"Tell me what you did!"

I'm pushing her down, pressing her down under my weight. I can almost smell the fear emanating from her. Sickly sour-sweet, like day-old sweat. It brings me sick satisfaction to see her frightened. All these years, I've been afraid of her, and now I get to inflict that misery back. I press her arms down towards the floor, enjoying her whimpers.

"Tell me!" I demand.

She stares at me like she doesn't recognise me. Her eyes are wide with incomprehension. But I don't trust it anymore. I don't trust a word she says.

"TELL ME!"

"I sold you."

"*What?*"

"We were starving, so I sold you."

I let her go. I stagger back, falling against the bed. This... This, I can't comprehend. What? What does she mean? I... I can't.

"Becca. I..." She's crying. I can hear it in her voice. I can't see her because I have my face in my hands, but I can hear it. "It was the most difficult decision of my life. Your father had committed suicide, leaving me in debt to loan sharks. We were about to lose the house. I knew we were going to be homeless in a matter of weeks. Your grandparents had cut me off and were refusing to see me or even speak to me." She pauses, but I can't bring myself to speak. So she continues. "It was in Geoff's old boozer that I found out you could do it. I was half-cut, chatting to one of his dodgy mates. He told me about these rich people who couldn't have kids of their own. He said they'd be willing to pay good money for a child, even more for twins, but I said no, I wouldn't get rid of my girls."

"But you did," I whisper.

"I felt sick all that day. I walked to the end of the street. I was coming for you. But I kept thinking about the mortgage. We were going to lose the house."

"You chose me. Out of everything you could have done. Out of begging, whoring yourself, stealing—you chose to sell *me*."

"They took the wrong one," she whispers.

"We switched our jumpers to trick Mrs Ellis at school."

"I never meant for—"

"She could be in the sex trade. She could have been sold to paedophiles and made to take drugs—"

"No," Mum interrupts. "It was a rich family in America who wanted to adopt but couldn't because of the paperwork. He told me."

"And you believed the word of a man who trafficked little girls? Did you?" I shout. "You believed that scum. I can't believe... I can't believe any of this." The truth is even worse than I could have imagined. My mother is a monster.

The rage finally hits me, seeping into every pore and filling me up. It becomes a living thing that grows and expands, taking the place of my organs and my veins, plugging my heart and soul with its dirty need. It demands an outlet. I grab hold of a cushion from the end of the bed and dive towards my monster of a mother.

She gasps and leans away from me. I hold the cushion an inch from her face with my heart pounding hard. Her eyes plead up to me.

I could end this in a few minutes. I could end it all. I would be free.

"Do it."

At first I think the voice came from Mum, but then I realise that her lips never moved. Then I think I whispered it to myself.

I didn't.

The voice came from the doorway to the bedroom. I drop the cushion, and I turn away to be face-to-face with the shadow that has been stalking me for the last few months.

PART TWO

CHAPTER TWENTY-TWO

ADELINE

Who shall I be today?

There's Boyfriend Guy in Brooklyn who thinks I'm plain old Katie. Good little Katie. She'll cook macaroni and make his bed. She brightens up his dingy apartment with her glowing smile and leaves her panties drying over the side of the tub. Then there's Summer Guy in the Hamptons who thinks I'm Serena, a girl from old money who dresses in pearls but gets dirty at night. And then I'm Roxanne for Party Guy, getting fucked up on Molly. Then we get fucked up on each other until the sun rises.

To Mom and Dad, I was always Addy. They didn't know about the others. I was their sweet miracle Addy who came to them when they thought they'd never have children. But they're gone now.

At their funeral I wasn't Addy anymore, at least not to them. I was Adeline Burke, the grieving daughter, forced to hug and shake the hands of all the men who could easily have killed her parents. But none of them did, and I should know.

Daddy tried to hide it, but I knew what he did. I used to sneak into his office and read his papers, carefully remembering the order and position of each one. His office was private, but I knew where he hid a spare key to get in. I knew about his schemes. I knew his corruption went beyond money laundering, beyond Wall Street, beyond politics. He was a criminal, but he was a criminal with connections, and—more importantly—money.

I was being Roxanne with Party Guy when I heard about Mom and Dad's car crash. I'm with him again when Ralph calls. Daddy's lawyer.

Party Guy has a trust fund, part of which went towards his Upper West Side apartment overlooking Central Park. It's late afternoon when I wake, bleary-eyed, to the sound of my cell phone. It's getting harder to be party girl Roxanne. Now that I'm in my thirties, it's getting harder to be any of my alter egos. I might be able to keep Serena for a few more summers. Katie is getting tiresome, anyway.

I wonder when I'll get to be Adeline?

My phone is hidden under Party Guy's jeans,

tossed between his sofa and the TV.

"Yes."

"Adeline, it's Ralph."

"Hey, Ralphio."

"We need to go over your parents' wills. Can you get to my office at, say, 9am tomorrow?"

I groan. "Does it have to be so early? You're a goddamn sadist, Ralphie."

I imagine him smiling. His eyes started to wander to my intimate places after I hit fifteen and my breasts began to blossom. To me, he's looked fifty for the last twenty years, probably because he's been overweight and balding all that time. There's a rustle on the other end of the line, and I know he's reached for a napkin or handkerchief to mop his sweaty brow. I've thought about fucking Ralph a few times, mainly to piss off Daddy, and partly because I *can*. But I never did. I wonder if it was the thought of those sweaty handkerchiefs that put me off.

"We need to get it sorted out, Addy. You're inheriting a lot of money. We need to discuss your trust fund and potential investments. We need to talk about your father's business."

"I told you, I'm not taking it over. I'm not running it. I just want the money." Translation: I don't want the hassle of the Feds snooping through my finances. They've been lurking for years. They know Daddy was dirty, but he was always quicker and smarter. They never got even close to catching him.

"Yeah, I know. But you're still coming in to talk to me. 9am sharp."

The corner of my mouth turns up. I like it when he's bossy. It's like Daddy's still here. "All right. Don't get your panties in a bunch. I'll be there."

"Good girl."

Party Guy rolls over and moans. I pat him on the forehead, gather my clothes, and light a cigarette on the way out.

"I hope you weren't smoking in the elevator again," the doorman admonishes. "One of these days, Roxie…"

"It's cool. I put my hand over the sensor."

"Have a good day, now." He grins as he opens the door for me.

I give him a wink on the way out, and that grin only widens.

It's 4pm and the city is bustling. I haven't eaten all day and my head is thumping, so I pick up strong coffee and a pretzel. I could call my driver, but I'd rather get the subway back to Tribeca. Daddy wanted me to move to Fifth Avenue, but I didn't fit in with the Fifth Avenue crowd. I don't want to stand out. I like the feeling of melting into the background so I can be no one. New York is perfect for that.

So, who should I be today? Should I be Adeline? The woman without a purpose, without a direction? A woman who for some reason has lived to be thirty-five and still doesn't feel whole? Or should I be no one, disappearing into the crowds on the subway, waiting for the next mask to wear? Yes, I think I'll be that person.

*

Ralph Scalzi sits behind a mahogany desk. A stereotypical show of masculine power. I've often wondered if the overcompensation of large cars for small-dicked men applies to desks, too. It wouldn't surprise me, not with Ralph. But then, he's always tried to appear bigger, more imposing than he really is.

Scalzi, the genius lawyer—if there's a loophole, he'll find one; if there's a favour to be cashed in, he'll do it—has worked with high-ranking mobsters, corrupt politicians, and crooked businessmen. And my father, who could be considered a little of all of the above. But he's a small man with a large frame—short and squat—and a face that reddens at even the slightest of exertion. Whenever I meet with him, I can't get rid of the mental image of him huffing and puffing on top of me. It used to make me giggle. But now I see him and imagine what my future could bring. Party Guy could soon be a thing of the past, replaced with Sweaty, Balding Guy.

I shudder.

"Addy, you made it. And look at that, only five minutes late." He gestures to the chair in front of his desk.

"It's a personal record."

"How are you doing?"

I let out a sigh. Ralph should know better than to ask me that. He isn't one of the pitying many who tilt their heads at me when they mention my parents. I'm not that person. I'm not someone to ever be pitied.

"I'm fine."

"If you need anything—"

I put up my hands, cutting him off. "I'm fine."

I can't help but notice how his eyes trail down past the cleavage revealed by the loose-fitting red dress I threw on this morning. To give Ralph some credit, those wandering eyes have never ceased, not even after I turned thirty. Most men seemed to lose interest after I hit the big 3-0. I haven't gotten as many free drinks, despite keeping my figure all these years. I've often wondered if Ralph is harbouring more than just a secret boner for my body. I wonder if he'd had real feelings for me over the years. I also wonder what his wife would think about that.

He shuffles his papers, and a ripple of tension works along his jaw. Ralph isn't exactly easygoing, but he seems even more tense than usual today. A bead of sweat runs along his temple. He starts to reach for the handkerchief in his top jacket pocket, then thinks better of it and clears his throat. "Addy, there's a lot to talk about today. There are things in your parents' wills that I have to tell you, and they might come as a shock."

I feign surprise. "Daddy was a crook. I already

know that. Were they in debt? Did they spend all the money?"

"No, it's nothing like that. And you can't say anything like that about your father in this room. I'm your lawyer, remember?"

I shrug. "Sure. So, what's the big deal? What's going on with Daddy's money?"

"Oh, it's nothing to do with that. Both your mother and father left you a substantial amount in your trust fund, along with the apartment on the Upper East Side and the summer house in Southampton. The details are all in the will. What I wanted to talk to you about is your adoption."

"My adoption?" I lean forward in the chair. "What? But I didn't... I didn't know."

Ralph fingers a manila envelope. He taps the desk twice, something I've noticed he does as a nervous tic. "What I'm about to tell you is information that even I didn't learn until after your parents' death."

Now I'm interested.

"You see, your father couldn't have told me while he was alive because it would have been admitting a felony to me. You weren't adopted, Adeline. You were bought."

The word hits me like a fist. *Thwack.* I was *bought*?

For once, I'm speechless. Mom used to say it would take a miracle to shut me up; that I came out of the womb talking. Huh. I guess that was a lie too.

"The details of the... err... sale are in this envelope. All I know is that your father paid a group of men to smuggle you into the country from England. Your parents lived upstate at the time. Your mother had a criminal record, which is why they could never adopt legally. When your parents moved away from their old life, they passed you off as their own and registered you as their child. Strings had to be pulled, apparently, but it wasn't me who arranged it all."

I lean back in my chair, blown sideways by the news. The Molly and the alcohol from the other night must be catching up with me, because my stomach is roiling like an old washing machine.

"I can't believe this. So, where do I come from?"

He passes me the envelope. "London. From a single parent who couldn't afford to keep you. Arrangements were made for you to be snatched from a park and smuggled into the country."

A low, simmering rage builds up from my churning gut. I haven't felt that for a long time, and it frightens me. I clench and unclench my fist, trying to keep the beast in check. "And how much did I cost? How much did this woman get?"

Ralph squirms in his seat. "I don't know."

I rip open the envelope and begin to thumb through the contents. I glance up at Ralph. "Know any good private detectives?"

CHAPTER TWENTY-THREE

ADELINE

Daddy was a tall man. Mom always said that was one of the reasons that people trusted him. Men are meant to be tall. They're meant to tower over women and command respect. That doesn't mean women have to be weak. There are Amazons among us. There are also quietly fierce women you wouldn't mess with. Mom could have been one of those women, if she hadn't met my father. She grew up on scraps in a poverty-stricken family of seven kids. She was hooked on drugs until she met Daddy and he got her clean, but not before she'd been in and out of jail.

You see, Daddy loved nothing more than a wounded bird, and that's why I know it's all true. He would've loved the idea of taking in a child unloved enough to be sold by her own mother.

Since my meeting with Ralph, I've had the same dream over and over again. I'm little, about five years old, I'm tired and hungry and self-conscious of how bad I smell. There's a tall man staring at me, a man with blue eyes. He's talking to me.

"We're going to have to get rid of that accent."

I reply, but I can't hear the words.

"Loud little thing. You've got some spunk, don't you?"

I can't remember if I agreed or disagreed.

I didn't feel anything when my parents died. You see, Daddy loved wounded birds, but he liked breaking them, too. It was a cycle with him. The women in his life should be broken, then fixed, then broken again. He liked them broken more, so that they never got ahead of themselves.

And Mom never did anything to stop it. I guess she had her own problems when Daddy drank too much and beat her, but she never left him and she never stopped him. She deserved it.

I grew up all broken inside. What scares me more than anything in this world is that all the pieces that are broken up inside me will one day come to the surface and everyone will see who I really am. They screwed me up bad, which is why I figured I might as well get some money out of it all. They broke me, but I killed them.

It was a hit and run.

But I know who to pay. I know which palms to grease with the dirty money Daddy earned for me. I should have done it years ago. I should have paid for my freedom. It's only now that I realise what he took from me. What he bought.

It's time to find the women who broke me first. According to the envelope Ralph gave me, my real name is Sophie Howland and I was born in suburban London to Maureen and Geoff Howland. My father committed suicide four years after I was born. Maureen sold me a year after that. But it gets worse. The part that I can't wrap my head around is that I have a twin sister named Becca Howland.

A twin.

There are no pictures. That's what I want more than anything: to see the face of the mother who sold me to the highest bidder. The woman who didn't care if I ended up in the sex trade, or was sold to a man who liked to break the will of little girls. She simply didn't care.

Ralph gives me the number of a John Ashley, a private detective he trusts. If Ralph trusts him, I trust him. To a point, anyway. There isn't a human being on this Earth that I trust with my whole heart.

I arrange it all over the phone, though I'm desperate to know what this John Ashley looks like. I prefer to be able to imagine the people I'm speaking to; otherwise the suspense becomes too much. I resolve to Google him on the internet once I'm off the phone.

It's a fairly simple transaction. I give him the details about Maureen Howland and wire him a bunch of money. He tells me he'll be in touch. And then I wait.

Except I don't.

I do my own digging. I put the name Maureen Howland into Facebook and set the parameters to London. There are a few dozen profiles, but only five or six are the right age. Most have their accounts set to private, showing little more than their profile pictures. I have no way of knowing which of them could be my mother, so I decide to hate them all with the same ferocity.

Then I try Becca Howland. I scour every profile, but none of them resemble me, so I shut down the computer and pace the apartment.

There's someone out there walking and talking and looking like me. Is she more comfortable in my skin than I am? Has she had the life I deserved? Has she been loved and cuddled and tucked in at night? Safe and warm in the true love of a mother?

I can't stand knowing she's out there.

*

My dreams change. I no longer dream about the first moment I met Daddy. I dream about *her*. Becca. We're in school, at the back of the classroom. I remember the hole in my shoe that let in water, and the wonky home haircut I used to sport. Becca and I had almost identical wonky hair because our mother always used to veer to the right with her scissors. I remember that now. It's a small piece of knowledge that I *knew*, but hadn't accessed for years.

In my dreams, we're at the back of the classroom and our heads are bent low so that we can whisper to each other. We're giggling. We have an idea.

"One, two, now you," I say.

That's our cue. It's our code that means we're about to do a dare. This time, while the teacher has her back to us, we whip off our sweaters and swap them. Then we swap places. For the rest of the class, I'm Becca and she's Sophie. I'm beaming, full of glowing confidence, because I know that Becca wants to be me. Everyone does. I make people laugh and smile. I can get people to do things for me by being cheeky.

"Come on, Shadow," I say to Becca as we wait outside the school gates. "If we don't hurry up, they'll make us wait inside the school and Mum will get in trouble."

"I don't know if we should," Becca replies.

I take her hand in mine and lead her away from the school.

That's when I wake up in a puddle of my own sweat. I don't like these dreams. I don't like remembering that I had a relationship with my sister, one that contained a great deal of affection. I press my knuckles against my skull, wishing all the memories away. But they won't go. They plague me.

It's a week before John Ashley calls me. I meet with him immediately, no longer able to stand the suspense. I sit in his office on Long Island, tapping his desk with a pen, full of enough nervous energy for stadium full of virgins on prom night.

He takes an obscene amount of time to get his papers together before he begins. While he's jerking around I study him, relieved to finally know what he looks like. He's younger than I imagined, maybe late forties, very fuckable. Maybe if I ditch Party Guy, I'll have a spot open for PI Guy. I like the chestnut stubble on his chin, and his big, strong hands.

"Your birth mother moved away from London shortly after your disappearance. She moved to a small village in North Yorkshire called Eddington."

He pushes a photograph across the desk, and I finally get to see her. I snatch it greedily, hungry for knowledge.

"Can I keep this?" I ask.

"Of course."

The photograph is grainy. There's a chance that it's a selfie, judging by the angle of the picture. That in itself is odd, that my birth mother is the kind of person who would take a selfie of herself, probably for social media. The resemblance hits me instantly. I've never noticed how much I don't resemble my parents—until I see how much I do resemble my real mother. We have the same sharp eyes and high cheekbones. She holds herself like some old-time queen, staring down at the peasants below. If I didn't hate her, I might like her.

"That's from her Facebook account," John continues.

"But I checked Facebook, and I couldn't find her," I say.

"It was a tricky process. She'd removed her profile from appearing on the search. After I learned that she'd moved to Eddington, I trawled through the friends lists of women her age in the area. Eventually she popped up."

I nod. "What about Becca Howland?"

John's eyes flash, and for the first time I realise he loves his job. "Ahh, well, that was a lot more... interesting. According to your father's records, you are Sophie Howland, which means your sister must be Becca Howland. You're the girl snatched from a park in 1985. But there must have been a mistake, because your birth mother registered *Becca* Howland as missing. The disappearance hit the newspapers in England. Your parents were lucky that you were never discovered. A week after you were taken, another child went missing and people lost interest."

"But I have memories from when I was a child, and I *remember* being Sophie. I'm not Becca. Becca was my sister."

"Becca is definitely the child who was reported missing." He hesitates. "And later declared dead."

"She lied." My voice is hoarse and quiet. "She lied to the police. Why would she do that?"

John Ashley swallows before he replies. For the first time, he seems uncomfortable. He even pities me. I can see it in his eyes and in his slight, sympathetic frown. "I don't know."

"Do you have a picture of her?" I ask.

"Yes. I took it from the website for Eddington Primary School, where she works as a teacher. She doesn't have any social media accounts. Oh, except for a dating profile."

That almost makes me chuckle. The thought of my sister dating internet guys. But my desire to laugh is killed when I'm holding the photograph of her in my hand.

The punch to my stomach is so hard I can't breathe. I remember her now. I remember the sad little expression she'd get when I tricked her into covering up for me when I was naughty. I remember that her favourite stuffed toy was a lion missing an eye and stuffing coming out of his left paw. I remember how I pulled off his head once in a rage and Mum... Maureen... had to stitch it up. I remember how my sister's voice sounded exactly like mine, and we both had a London accent. I remember her smell and the feel of her hair.

There are sobs caught in my throat, which feels ridiculous as I stare down at this woman who seems little more than a sad version of me. Her haircut is bad, her teeth are wonky, and there are lines around her eyes that I don't have. She's heavier than I am. Her posture is slouched forward, making her breasts appear to be sagging.

"Would you like a tissue?" John Ashley holds out the tissue box, but I shake my head. "It's a lot to take in, isn't it? You have a whole other family that you never knew about."

"A family that sold me and stole my identity." I sniff heavily and force the tears back. "Have you got an address for them?"

CHAPTER TWENTY-FOUR

ADELINE

At 20,000 feet, the bleach-blonde woman still wearing her sunglasses finally turns to me and says, "We don't get many Americans coming to Manchester from New York. It's usually us tourists going home."

"I'm going home to visit family. They live in Yorkshire."

"Oh, how funny." When she laughs, her sunglasses bob up and down on her nose. She has a voice that grates. Almost nasal.

"They're distant relations. I hardly know them." I lean back into the leather seat. I thought about flying cattle class to avoid attention, but then I figured that no one would be paying much attention to me anyway. It's not like *Maureen* and *Becca* will be watching out for me. I've been gone for thirty years.

"Well, that calls for a bit of a celebration, then, doesn't it? Fancy a glass of prosecco?"

"Make it champagne and you're on," I reply.

"I'm Amy, by the way," she says.

I try to get a good view of her, but with the sunglasses I can't quite guess her age. Her hair is dyed well enough to cover any grey, and her body is petite. She's wearing expensive, if trashy, designer clothing, favouring animal print and black.

"Sophie," I reply. I savour the name, feeling it on my tongue and sliding over my teeth. It slips out, smooth as melted toffee. I'm still not quite ready to be *her*, but I like trying the name on for size. "Tell me, Amy, do people in North Yorkshire speak like you?"

"You mean the accent? It's close, but not quite. You'll see when you get there."

"Can you teach me a few sentences to say in your accent? I'll teach you New York."

The stewardess brings over two champagne flutes, and Amy giggles.

"All right, then. How about, 'Fancy a cuppa, love?'" I repeat the phrase, and she laughs. "Not bad!" I try it again, and her eyebrows rise above the rim of her enormous glasses. "Hey, you're getting good at this."

"I'm pretty good at picking up accents," I reply.

"No kidding."

*

Amy is kind enough to tell me about the "high street shops" in England and where to buy the dowdiest clothes. I tell her they're for my aunt, but I want to try on the clothes "Sophie" wears.

I rent a car in Manchester and practice driving on the wrong side of the road along some smaller, residential streets where dirty children are kicking soccer balls around. The car is a Ford Focus, something Daddy would never rent—or drive, or ride in. It's old compared to the cars I used to drive when I ventured out of Manhattan. It's a dull grey, exactly what I need to blend into the scenery.

England strikes me as a pretty grey place. The sun only seems to come out in patches. Then it disappears back behind the clouds, and the sky goes back to gloom.

On the drive to Yorkshire, I listen to an audiobook set in the very same county, pausing every so often to repeat the phrases. I stop in a pub for dinner and change into my new clothes. The bra fits badly, making my breasts feel unsupported. I don't bother to brush my hair, and I slump forward a little. I wash away the last traces of my make-up. I'm almost her.

When I order my food I try out the new accent, taking care to listen closely to the way the young waitress speaks. If she notices my phoney accent she doesn't mention it; she doesn't even look at me funny. She comes back promptly with my large cheeseburger and fries, which I already knew were called chips. I need to put some weight on if I'm going to be her. We're the same, but not quite. She's had thirty years of British food and dentistry. I've had thirty years of Upper East Side New York.

My stomach tingles with the thought of those two differing histories finally colliding in what can only be a monumental event. I eat my burger and repeat the address of Maureen and Sophie Howland over and over in my mind.

I decide to stay at a small bed and breakfast in the town nearest to Eddington. There are a few vacation cottages in Eddington itself, but I'd rather not draw attention to myself. Plus, there's the added fear of being mistaken for Sophie before I'm ready.

Upstairs in my room, I stare at the picture of Sophie and walk around the room pretending I'm her. Before I drifted into apathy, I took some acting classes, and I even auditioned for a few plays. Daddy was never happy about me being an actress. He was adamant that it wasn't the right career path. We argued about it for a while. Mom even tried to talk me out of it.

They needn't have bothered. I was neither talented nor beautiful enough to be an actress, as pretty much every agent in New York told me.

But the joke has been on them for the last fifteen years, because I've discovered how to become someone else, and isn't that the ultimate acting job?

The Yorkshire accent becomes how I think. It's time to rid my vocabulary of the word "mom". Maureen Howland is my *mum*. She's fifty-five years old, and she lives in Eddington. When I was five years old, she sold me to my mother and father for an undisclosed sum of money.

No, I can't think like that. I'm the *other* Sophie Howland, the one who has grown up in a small house in Eddington and who has never moved away from that same village. She's stuck by her mother's side all these years, even living in the same house, without finding a husband or having children of her own, and she works at an elementary—no, primary school, teaching children in her Marks and Spencer cardigans.

Sophie Howland has never left the country. She's never walked around Central Park out of her mind on ecstasy at 4am or tried to chew her own cheek off on the subway.

I lie down on my lumpy bed and wonder what she's doing right now. It's the first time that doubt creeps in. What if all this goes wrong? What if I lose control of the situation and I'm the one who ends up hurt? But my mind keeps returning to the day that I led Becca—or *Sophie,* as she's calling herself now—out of the school gates, and I was snatched away. I was robbed of a sister. Robbed of spending my teenage years arguing over clothes and who to take to the prom.

Do they even *have* proms in England? Who cares. I missed all that stuff. I miss it now. I miss her.

*

I programme Eddington into the GPS on my rental car and drive over to the village. The place is how I imagined all of England to be, filled with small houses and gardens, all identical and quaint. It's immediately obvious that this place is more affluent than some of the other towns I've driven through to get here. A shiver of rage runs up my spine, heating my face and fingers. *I* paid for this. It was the sale of *me* that allowed Maureen to move her one remaining child here.

The first time I see the house, I almost pull over to vomit, but the urge recedes, thankfully. There's nothing strange about the house. It's the same as any other. There it is, the place where my sister lives as me, and my mother treats her like she would have treated me. Why did she swap our identities? I don't believe for a moment that she mixed us up. The vague memories I have of her tell me that she never mixed us up. She always knew which of us was which. The teachers at school could never tell, but she did.

I park the car across the street and sit low in my seat, tucking my hair into a hat. It's Saturday morning, and I don't know their routine. I don't know if they'll even come out of the house, but my heart thumps at the thought of seeing one of them for the first time.

"Come on, Shadow," I whisper.

I watch as a petite woman with cropped blonde hair, wearing a nurse's uniform, walks down the street. She turns the corner onto Maureen and Sophie's driveway and raps on the door. Now my heart is in my mouth. I'm about to catch a glimpse of at least one of them. I don't even think about why a nurse would come to their house; I'm too busy concentrating on the thought of seeing them. Will it be Maureen? Or will it be Sophie?

The door opens wide, and I gasp.

It's *her*. Sophie. The woman who looks like me. I hear her voice.

"Hi, Erin. Thanks for coming on a Saturday..."

It's *my* voice, except it isn't. I commit it to memory. There's a twang of the Yorkshire accent I've been practising, but it isn't quite as strong as I thought it would be. I repeat her words softly to myself.

Hi, Erin. Thanks for coming on a Saturday.

The sight of her is another punch to the gut. All these years I've been grieving the loss of her, but I put it out of my mind. Mom and Dad always told me that I never had a sister, that I used to be friends with someone a long time ago and it's that friend I remember. After a while I put it all out of my mind and started my new life without ever looking back.

Do I regret that? No. I needed to survive. I needed to move forward.

And now I need more. I need answers, and I

need justice.

CHAPTER TWENTY-FIVE

ADELINE

It's easy to stay at the B&B without raising any suspicions. I pay for a month up front and tell the friendly woman who runs the place that I'm keeping a low profile after leaving an abusive husband. She taps her nose and replies, "Say no more." So I don't.

I learn Sophie's routine. She waits until the blonde nurse, Erin, gets to the house every weekday morning, and then she drives to Eddington Primary School. She leaves between 4 and 5pm every day and comes home. Erin leaves around ten minutes later. Maureen barely leaves the house.

There has to be a reason why Maureen needs constant care. I keep watching. Sometimes on the weekend Maureen and Sophie go shopping together, or go to a café.

I have to be very careful when I follow them. At one point I switch rental cars to a blue Nissan to stop any nosy neighbours from getting suspicious. The street is fairly quiet, but it's also close to a park that seems popular with parents who like to drive everywhere. That means the neighbours are accustomed to seeing strange cars on the street. But when Sophie and Maureen leave the house, I have my hair tied back and tucked under a hat. The weather is hot and sunny, which makes the hat uncomfortable, but at least my sunglasses don't stick out like a sore thumb.

After Sophie has left for work, I sneak around to the back of the house and watch as Maureen comes out to the garden. I watch as she settles into a deck chair with a cup of tea. After taking a sip, she throws the tea to the ground, breaking the mug on the patio stones.

Erin comes rushing out into the garden. "Oh, what did you do that for?" she says with a sigh.

"It was too hot."

"I did say to let it cool."

After Erin is done cleaning up the mess, Maureen says, "Where's my cup of tea? I asked for one hours ago."

"Give me two minutes, Maureen."

"Who are you, and where's Sophie?" Maureen snaps.

"I'm Erin. I'm your nurse. I've been taking care of you for a couple of months now. Do you remember?"

Maureen narrows her eyes as though she's trying to remember. "Yes. Yes, I think I do."

"I'll bring you that cup of tea."

As Erin walks away, I watch Maureen playing with a set of keys. She dangles them through her fingers and drops them onto the patio stones. Of course... the woman has dementia. That's why she needs a nurse.

Slowly, I pull the hat from my head and fluff out my hair. My heart is thumping against my ribs. I only have a few minutes while Erin is busy making the tea in the kitchen. I glance up at the kitchen. Erin has her back to the window.

Am I going to do this? I've done some risky things in my time, but this?

I open the gate into the garden and walk slowly up to Maureen.

"You dropped these, Mum. Maybe I should hold on to them for safekeeping."

A thrill passes through me as Maureen's eyes meet mine. "Yes, all right."

"I have to get back to work."

When she reaches out and grabs my hand, an electric shock jolts up my arm. I try hard to suppress the urge to rip my hand away from her.

"Wait. Are you—?"

"I'm Sophie, Mum."

She lets me go. Her eyes are unfocussed and confused.

I hurry back to the end of the garden, my breath

ragged and my forehead clammy. My fingers shake when I open and close the gate. I retrieve the hat from where I hid it and run to my car. I drive away, and I contemplate never coming back.

*

My room at the B&B smells like vomit.

I haven't done that since I paid that guy to drive into my father's Mercedes. It's true that I felt numb when my parents died, but when I hired the hit man, I reacted more strongly than I'd ever thought I would.

I hold the keys until the metal warms. Now I can get into their house. After I've purged myself of the loathing hiding in my belly, a new kind of excitement tickles my empty stomach. I took some of the control from Maureen. They can never get that back.

But I need to be careful. Sophie will hunt for these keys when she realises Maureen has lost them. She might even change the locks. Tomorrow, I'll get replicas made of every key, and then I'll toss the keys back into the garden. Maureen will barely even realise they've been gone. And if she tells Sophie about seeing me—or rather, *her*—Sophie will put it down to her dementia. She'll never believe her.

*

When I was fifteen, I broke into an old movie director's house in the Hamptons with my friend Jake. We wanted to have sex in his pool. We climbed over the wall, and I fell heavily on the ground and hurt my ankle. Before I knew it, there were lights everywhere and a huge guy jumped on top of me while I wriggled and giggled, high on whatever drugs we'd found lying around Jake's parents' house.

It was my one and only attempt at breaking and entering. Until now.

The Howland house is silent. I slip in through the garden gate and around the path to the front of the house. I didn't want to walk up to the front door in case any of the neighbours happened to be staring out of their window in the middle of the night, but the sliding doors to the garden will make too much noise.

I know from watching the house that there isn't an alarm. There's no dog. I have the key. I just need to be silent.

I'm wearing all black, including a black balaclava. I'm a real criminal now.

I slide the key into the lock and twist it slowly. The sound of the door opening is quieter than my hammering heart. I don't quite close the door, because I know I'll need to escape fast if anyone wakes up.

My shoes are silent against the carpet. When my eyes have adjusted to the gloom, I scan the living room of the house I might have grown up in. What if Maureen hadn't sold me and had gotten the money to move to Eddington some other way? This is the sofa I would have sat on to watch Molly Ringwald movies with my sister. That's the kitchen I would have made grilled cheese in, or whatever they call it here. Maybe beans on toast, then.

Maybe I would have been able to convince Mum to get us a dog. We could have played with him in the garden when we weren't arguing about boys.

There's no other option than to shut down my thoughts. I have jobs to do. The most important is logging on to Sophie's computer. I want to know everything I can about the two of them. But first, I have to install software to allow me to control her laptop from my own, which will be impossible if her laptop is password protected.

I open the machine on the kitchen table and suppress the urge to let out a sigh of relief when it opens onto her desktop automatically. I quickly insert a USB stick and install the remote desktop software. There's an agonising minute or two when I can do nothing but wait. Then I put the laptop back in position and slip the USB stick back into my pocket.

At the bottom of the stairs, I imagine the two of them sleeping softly, with no idea that I'm in their house. Before I know it, my feet are moving up the stairs. A slight creak from the floorboards forces me to stop. Without breathing, I listen to the house. I hear it settle, but there's no indication that either Sophie or Maureen has woken. I take the last few steps slowly.

I have no idea who sleeps in which room. It's by pure chance that I gently open the door closest to the stairs to find the woman who gave birth to me sleeping quietly on her side with her mouth slightly agape. There she is, the woman who held a baby girl in her arms and then five years later sold that child to corrupt men for them to do with her whatever they wanted. I could have been sold to a paedophile ring or worked as a sex slave for the rest of my life. I could have been murdered for pleasure and left in an unmarked grave. Would I have found more peace in that unmarked grave than in the life I have now?

This woman robbed me of so many things, and there isn't enough money in Daddy's trust fund to make up for that. I reach towards her, stopping an inch from her face. A few minutes and I could take her last breath.

Her eyes open.

I retract my hand. I pull the ski mask from my face so she can see me.

"Sophie?" she says.

"You know what you should do?" I say. "You should drink bleach. An entire bottle. You should take all your pills at once. It would make you better."

"Okay," she mumbles.

I turn away and hurry out of the house, away from the family who abandoned me.

CHAPTER TWENTY-SIX

ADELINE

A few days ago, I saw Sophie meet a man for coffee. It was exhilarating for me, because it was the first time I had seen Sophie with someone who wasn't her mother or one of the teachers at school. Now able to access her laptop from my own in the B&B bedroom, I discovered that this man's name was Peter and that he had been messaging her on her dating profile. Things seemed pretty serious, judging from his messages, though Sophie clearly wasn't as interested as he was.

I broke into the Howland house a few times after the first try. It was too easy—and it was addictive. Sophie, clearly a heavy sleeper, never woke while I crept up the stairs and whispered to our mother in the darkness.

"I know you," she said to me once.

"You will know me," I replied.

Every morning, when I watch Sophie go to work, she appears even more exhausted than before. She's had to take our mother to the hospital after Maureen drank the bleach, an event that made me excited and sick at the same time. She had to call the police and change the locks. That was disappointing. If I try to steal Maureen's keys again, it might be noticed. My days of letting myself into the house at night are over. Especially after Sophie installs CCTV cameras.

But then she does something even better. She's installed hidden cameras in her own home that she can access on her computer. Which means I can access them too.

I see everything. I see their daily lives. Every dull evening spent on the sofa in front of the TV. Every time Maureen throws a tantrum at her nurse. Every time Sophie pours herself a glass of wine and puts her head in her hands at the end of the day. I see it all.

So I mess with them. I ruin Sophie's relationship with the nurse. Why should she get to have best friends? I sleep with her boyfriend. He doesn't even realise it isn't her. He's fat and unattractive, but I'm so turned on by the thought of being *her* that I don't care. I find a bag of clothes meant for charity sitting on the front step. After stealing one or two items, I cut the rest into ribbons.

I know where every camera is, inside and outside the house. I can turn some of them off via the software I installed on Sophie's laptop. I do it just to freak her out. The thought of messing with her head, making her paranoid, becomes so exhilarating and addictive that I can't stop.

Whatever they do, I'm watching. When they get undressed at night, I'm watching. In those lonely moments of devastation, when nothing but alcohol-driven tears will do, I'm watching. They can't escape me. I'm back, despite their best efforts to forget me, and I'll make sure that they know me, once and for all.

During this time of prying into their intimate moments, what I find the most interesting are Sophie's emails to her ex-boyfriend, Jamie. It gives me an insight into a facet of Sophie and Maureen's relationship that I didn't know existed. It seems that Maureen didn't just rob me of the childhood I deserved, she withheld that childhood from my sister. I can see it through every word in those emails. I see the complete and utter destruction of self-confidence in my sister. I see the toxic relationship that exists between her and our mother, and the way it breaks her relationship with Jamie.

I go through all of her emails, creating screen shots and printing them out. I pin them to my hotel wall, highlighting important sections:

I can't do this anymore, Soph. I can't watch her pick you apart bit by bit. I can't have children with you because I don't want her as their grandmother.

You need to stand up to her or you'll never be free.

Put her in a home, Sophie. Sell the house. Move in with me and be happy.

It's so urgent and desperate. As a child, I watched Mom and Dad drunkenly tear chunks from one another. I saw them bruised black and blue from each other's rage, but I never saw anything so sad as this long, tiresomely polite deconstruction of frustration. It almost breaks my heart.

Almost.

But Sophie was given a choice. She could have left our mother long ago and lived a life of freedom. I'm still the one who was sold, and she's still the sister who stole my identity, leaving me with nothing.

It's not long after I've paid for my second month at the B&B that I decide that the time has come. The games are about to stop. I need to speak to my sister. I need to stop *being* her and *face* her.

PART THREE

CHAPTER TWENTY-SEVEN

It has been her this entire time.

The woman is mirror perfect.

But I don't see her. I see the girl I lost all those years ago. There she is, the girl who was born before me, but only by seconds. I see her as the five-year-old girl with freckles across her nose. I see the itchy jumper she used to wear in the winter and her wicked grin when we tricked our teachers. Her eyes are as sparkly as they ever were. Her face is mine, and yet it not. It is the face I have wanted — needed — to see all these years. She's the other half of me that I've walked this world without. There she is. My sister.

Somehow it doesn't matter that she has stalked and humiliated me, that she has reduced me to a quivering wreck: a woman standing over her own mother with a pillow, trying to decide whether I'd rather be a free murderer, or a trapped victim.

She stands before me. She's here. She's going to show me what to do, like she did all those years ago.

She lifts her chin. "Hello, Shadow."

"I always hated that name." I swallow. "*Sophie*." It feels so right to say that name at last. Now I know why I've never felt comfortable in my own skin, why I've felt like an imposter my entire life. The reason is standing there in front of me, eclipsing me, turning me into a shadow. She was taken before I could find my way out of that shadow. I fell in behind my mother, and I never managed to claw my way out.

"Hello, *Mother*." Sophie's tone of voice is ice-cold. Her eyes, identical to mine, narrow into two hard slits. Is that what I look like when I'm angry? Do I ever scrunch up my nose in that way? Are her facial tics my facial tics? We would have compared ourselves as we grew up. We would have stared into the mirror and giggled about how similar we were. Or how different.

Immediately, I can understand how Mum could always tell us apart. Sophie stands in a way that makes people look up to her. I slouch into my knees so that everyone looks down at me.

"Sophie. You're… Is this real?" Mum's voice is quiet, breathless. She can't believe her own eyes. I'm not sure I can, either.

I move away from Mum so that she can sit up. There are traces of tears on her cheeks. She reaches forward as though to touch her long-lost daughter.

SARAH A. DENZIL

I watch as my sister's expression morphs into a grimace. Her tensed shoulders almost fill the doorway. My eyes follow the long line of her arm to discover the knife in her hand. Of course. This woman stalked me. She broke into my house. She hacked my email account and cut my clothes into ribbons. It dawns on me that she probably slept with Peter. *That's* why he turned up on the doorstep in such a disturbed state. She might even have killed our neighbour's cat.

I can't trust her.

Mum climbs unsteadily to her feet. "You're here, and you're real. I knew it. All these years, I knew it. And look at you. You're as beautiful today as you were when I let you go. You've had a good life, haven't you? They told me that the family was well off, that they'd provide for you better than I could."

The real Sophie lets out a derisive snort. "I've been provided for. Don't worry about that." Her voice is sarcastic. Mocking. I want to bite my lip and cower. Doesn't she know Mum's temper? Doesn't she know her sharp tongue?

Of course she doesn't.

"You went to the family they told me about. Thank God. When I never heard from them again, all kinds of thoughts ran through my mind." Mum hurries towards Sophie, but my sister cringes away from her. "What did they call you?"

Sophie recoils, shrinking back from the door. "Adeline."

Mum places a hand over her mouth. "Adeline.

264

So pretty."

I can't deny that it hurts me to see Mum treat this woman—who looks exactly like me—as anything other than the ugly, useless lump I've come to be. Why is Sophie... Adeline... so beautiful?

Mum reaches out, and Adeline allows her to run her fingers through her hair. Tears run down her chin.

"It was never supposed to be you," Mum whispers.

Adeline's eyes find mine. "That's not a nice thing to say to your daughter."

But Mum isn't listening. She's still touching Adeline's hair.

I lower myself onto the bed and place my head in my hands. It's only when the weight of the bed shifts that I lift my eyes to see Adeline sitting next to me.

"I wanted to be you," she says. "I found out about you after my parents died. They left me some information in an envelope informing me about what happened. I read that note, and I needed to know more. I needed to see you. I hired an investigator and dug into your lives. That's when I realised that you were living as Sophie. I thought you'd stolen my identity, the one that I should have had all those years ago."

"So, you stalked me?"

She glances away and continues, ignoring my question. "It didn't seem real. Part of me kept wondering whether it was all an elaborate hoax. But it made sense, because of who I am. The person I've grown up to be. Or not be."

She's the only one who understands. I've never been whole, but neither has she. I've never been Sophie, and she has never been Adeline.

"I never knew. The memories only started coming back to me recently, the first time I heard Mum say Shadow." Saying it out loud sends a ripple down my spine. Is it excitement? Fear?

"After my parents... the people who raised me... died, I started having dreams. Then pieces came back to me." She smiles. It seems genuine, and yet it's missing an essential humanlike quality. Warmth. "So, tell me. Have you felt like half a person, too?"

"Yes." The word is a breath.

"All because of her."

We turn to Mum.

It's Adeline doing the talking now, taking the lead as she did before she was snatched. "Tell us, Mum. What kind of mother sells one of her twin daughters before trying every other possible way to find money? I've heard extraordinary stories about women fighting for their children's survival. Mothers sacrifice themselves to shield their children from natural disasters, they prostitute themselves to earn money for their children, they fight in war-torn countries to get their children to a safer place. And yet your first thought was to sell one of us."

"It was never supposed to be you," Mum says.

This time, we don't react to that horrendous statement. We let her talk. We both want answers. This is our story. We have waited thirty years to hear it. We have been denied what was ours all along, and everything that has happened to us has come to this. We wait, and we listen.

"You were born first, Sophie. You were strong, healthy and beautiful. I gazed at your pink, round face, and for the first time in my life I felt what love is. Then I had to give birth to you, Becca." She regards me. "And you weren't easy. Not even from the beginning. You were born with the cord wrapped around your neck, and when the midwife tugged you out, you ruptured me. You wanted my blood right from the very beginning.

"You bruised my nipples from breastfeeding. You were always hungrier than Sophie, always needy and whining. The constant crying drove me mad. I started taking all the stress out on Geoff. Becca, you were all him. You had his temperament. Sophie searched for solutions to problems. She's a go-getter, someone who will always come out on top because life will never beat her down. You long for life to beat you down, Becca. You're the victim and you always will be, because that's the character you chose to play in life. I saw that when you were still in nappies. I knew it.

"Geoff was weak and stupid, and he gave up on life." She snarls when she says his name. "I married a man, but I buried a pathetic shell of a human being. He left me with nothing but debt. Gambling debt from a couple of loan sharks and a house I couldn't afford. If either of you have ever known the weight of debt, you'll know the kinds of decisions you have to make.

"I had no one to turn to. Don't look at me like that. Your father burned every bridge I had. My parents wouldn't even talk to me after I married that 'good-for-nothing' as Dad called him. I went to them once. They blanked me. Wouldn't even say hello. I had nothing, except for you both."

She folds her arms. "I made a bad decision."

Adeline entwines her fingers with mine. I flash back to that day in the park. The man who snatched her away from me looms over me. The strawberry lollipop hits the grass with a thud. My face is red and hot from screaming and flailing, reaching out and grabbing her hair. There was no one around who cared enough to come running in answer to my screams.

Maybe that's why I have always wanted a child. That's why I have ached for one, why I have felt as though I'd lost the child I'd never had. I went through the trauma of losing a child. I failed to protect my big sister, and she failed to protect me, too.

I think about how I became so attached to little Chloe and her imaginary friend. She reminded me of myself when I was a little girl grieving for my dead sister while being forced to forget all about her. I wanted to protect Chloe because I failed to protect Sophie when the kidnappers came to take her away.

"Becca, I can never forgive you," Mum continues. "Because of you, I lost my Sophie." She begins to cry. "But now I have her back. I can die, having seen her. When this disease takes me, I'll know that I've seen you, Sophie, and that you're safe."

When Adeline replies to this, her words are measured and calm, devoid of any emotion. A cold, creeping shiver worms its way up my spine. "You tried to sell one child and you ended up losing your favourite, so you forced the child you had left to be someone else and bullied her for years to come. You've never taken any responsibility for your actions, and you still blame Becca for what you did. I've met some despicable people. My parents weren't just rich, they were criminals. Why else would they need to buy a child? But you—you are the first person I've ever met who is truly broken inside. You're barely even a person. You're a monster."

I watch as the blood drains from Mum's face. She staggers back and slides slowly down the wall, ending up on her knees.

"We should call the police," I say.

"No," Adeline replies. "Not yet." She turns to me, and I can't help but gasp at the incredible likeness once again. "Becca, she was right about one thing. You do like to be a victim. You've stayed with this woman all your life, putting your own life on hold for someone who has so little love for you that she tried to sell you as a child. Where is your self-worth?"

"She beat it out of me a long time ago," I whisper.

"You're a grown woman," Adeline replies. "I'm sorry for what's happened to you, but I can never understand it."

The room is silent. Three women sit, and none of them look at each other.

It's me who breaks the silence. "You stalked me. You made me think that I was going insane. All this time, I thought it was Mum. I thought she was playing one last cruel joke on me before the Alzheimer's claims her."

Adeline starts to laugh. "You thought it was her? That's too perfect!"

"It's not funny!" I wrench my hand from hers.

The laughter stops. "Yes, it is."

"I'm going to call the police." I stand up, ready to retrieve my phone and end this charade.

But Adeline is quick to grasp my wrist. "No. That's not what's going to happen."

I frown at her. "What are you talking about? Mum needs to answer for what she did all those years ago. They could arrest the man who took you."

But Adeline shakes her head. "No."

She pulls me back onto the bed. I search her face for answers, but all I find is a blank mask.

"We have to," I whisper.

"No."

"Then, what?"

"I had something else in mind. But it doesn't involve the police." Adeline's voice is still as devoid of emotion as her expression. I wonder... How much of Mum is in Adeline?

"What happened to you after you were sold?" I ask. "Where did you go?"

"I went to New York," she says. "And I became a millionaire. It was the American dream in action. Becca. Sophie. My sister. I'm giving you a choice, and I want you to listen very closely. There's one reason I came to England, and it wasn't to catch up.

"I grew up around people who settled their differences in a very different manner. I've attended more funerals than weddings, and the last funeral was for my parents. The ones who bought me like a prize racehorse. You see, Daddy liked to break little girls, and Mommy liked to let it happen. It took me a while to figure out what I needed to do, but after I did it, I inherited millions of dollars. I'm quite willing to share those millions with you, little sis, but there's one thing you need to do for me first."

When she's grins at me, it's psychotic.

"What do you want me to do?" I force the words through a strangle-like grip on my throat. My mouth is bone-dry and my tongue is thick. The atmosphere in the room is as heavy as a brewing thunderstorm. I can taste the mildewed scent of the old photographs hanging around us, dripping with festering memories.

"I'm giving you a choice, which is more than Mum ever did for us. The choice is about life or death. Live, and come with me to New York, or die never leaving this grey, washed-out country."

"What?"

"Sounds like an easy choice, doesn't it? But there's more to it. I'm not leaving England until that woman over there is in the ground. So, if you want to live, you have to kill her. And if you won't do that, I'll kill you both."

She hands me the knife. "One. Two. Now *you*."

EPILOGUE

I'm a perfect mirror image.

At night, I remove my make-up bit by bit to reveal the woman underneath. There I am. I am here. I exist.

She was buried quietly on a grey, drizzly day, which she would have hated. I put little in the newspaper. I didn't want to attract attention. The cause of death was listed as suicide. At the funeral, I heard a few people discussing how only a few weeks before, she had tried to drink bleach. That made me smile. Loose ends all tied up nicely. No one will suspect the grieving daughter who stood by her side all these years.

I think I do a good impression of being her.

PC Hollis came to the funeral, which surprised me. Standing at the back of the meagre congregation, he was an unwelcome reminder of the last few months. It was easy enough to avoid him during the service. But I couldn't avoid him afterwards, when he traversed the damp grass of the cemetery to pass on his condolences.

Right away I saw the flash in his eyes and the tension along his jaw. He took my hand briefly, but soon dropped it. I was about to move away, but he began to speak.

"You never told me about your twin sister," he said.

"That..." I stuttered. "That was a part of our past that Mum kept private. She was ashamed... about the ordeal. She forgot to pick us up from school that day... and... well, you can understand."

"It would have helped greatly with the investigation." PC Hollis's eyes narrow.

I readjust the sunglasses on the bridge of my nose and angle my face down. His gaze is too penetrating, too searching. Too keen. He suspects something.

"I'm sorry I didn't mention it. With everything going on with Mum... You see, I started to think it was all in my head, that it was local kids messing around. I—"

"We both saw the footage, Ms. Howland. We both know that it wasn't teenagers. It was someone targeting you. Stalking you. With purpose."

"Well, they aren't anymore. I appreciate everything you've done for me, but you can drop the case. I've not had any prank callers, break-ins, or otherwise. Things are quiet as a mouse. Too quiet, now that Mum has gone. I'm sure you understand how much I miss her." I turn away sharply as my voice breaks.

"Of course. But there was another reason for me coming here today. I don't think we should close the case at all. The fingerprints weren't a match for you or your mother, but the prints were almost identical to yours. We believe they belong to your twin sister."

"What? Are you sure? But that's not possible. She was declared legally dead after seven years."

He nods slowly. I can tell that he's still searching my face for clues. He's checking to see whether I'm lying. My skin itches under his examination.

"I'm very sure."

I raise my hand to my mouth. Hollis's expression softens and he leans in, perhaps to comfort me with a touch, but I back away.

"This is all too much," I say through my fingers. My hand rises to wipe a tear from under my glasses. "It's my mother's funeral. I... I can't."

"I'm sorry to have caused you distress." For the first time, Hollis appears uncomfortable. He shifts his weight from one leg to the other and folds his arms. "I'd like to investigate this further. If we can find the whereabouts of your sister, Becca, I would love to bring her back for you."

"I have a lot on my plate right now. I'm sorting out the house and all the paperwork. Of course, that's what I want too. To see Becca. That would be... It would be a miracle. But you must understand that there have been many false alarms over the years, and there's a chance this could be one too."

Of course Hollis wants to find my sister. If he could close a thirty-year-old unsolved missing person case, he'd be a hero. And as for the false alarms, that's a lie. As far as I know, once my mother moved to Eddington, everyone forgot all about missing Becca. That wouldn't happen now, of course. Snatched children become newspaper fodder for decades.

I wonder what the news would make of my mother. I wonder how much money I would get for selling my story, like she sold a child...

Hollis takes my hand in his. "This is a good lead. I'm going to do everything I can, Sophie."

I believe him.

I need to act fast.

*

The day I finally close the door of that house for good, I actually visit her grave. The gravestone is black marble. It's small, with only a brief inscription. No "Loving Mother" or "Loyal Friend" or cutesy poem to show how much everyone cared. She died with no love from anyone, and she loved only one person in the world. If, in fact, it was love. Real love.

The English summer is fading as I climb into the

taxi. The early morning is cold, cloudy, and damp.

On the way, I ask the taxi driver to make a stop at a garage. There, I throw my phone into the courtyard bin. There are three missed calls: one from Alisha, and two from PC Hollis. I feel somewhat guilty about Alisha. But it's time to cast away this life. Soon, I will have to stop being her.

Hollis has been tricky. Luckily, I managed to fob him off with a brief meeting to go over the facts. He asked me about that September day thirty years ago, but I managed to lie.

While I was clearing out my mother's things from her bedroom, I came across a stack of newspaper clippings about the kidnapping. It was when reading through those that I came across "Sophie's" eyewitness statement. Sophie claimed that Becca ran away from her. There was no mention of the man in the park. The lies had my mother's influence written all over them. She knew that if the men were found, the trail would lead back to her. Once again, she put herself before her child. Once again, she proved to be selfish and narcissistic to her very core. I felt sick reading through those articles.

At least it gave me enough fodder to fool Hollis while I sold the house and got out of Eddington.

I almost drift into slumber as the taxi rolls on. I'm thankful that the driver isn't someone determined to fill silence with inane chatter. I'm grateful that he accepts the money and tip without asking me where I'm going or wishing me a good holiday.

The plane ticket burns a hole in my purse. The thought of it fills me with excitement.

The airport bustles. I weave my way through queues, metal detectors, and security.

They examine Sophie Howland's passport, and they say nothing. Only nod. And then I move on.

I'm given a boarding pass. Stickers are placed on my bag. I empty my make-up into transparent plastic bags and place them in a tray with my keys and the ereader I bought for the journey.

I'm ushered through a tunnel towards the enormous plane by a woman with perfect teeth. And, finally, I'm shown to my seat.

As I place my bag into the overhead compartment, my thoughts drift back to PC Hollis. I might not be free. Not yet. Once I've reached my destination, once I've put an ocean between me and that interfering man, I might be able to relax.

I keep thinking of the chances of him pursuing this case further. Is he a man to cut his losses and move on? Or will I be running from him for the rest of my life?

There are other people to consider. Peter—that creepy idiot—has not tried to get in contact. My phone is gone, I've left little trace behind, and I don't think he has the brains to find me. Alisha might try, but she has a family to worry about. Then there's Jamie, who hasn't been in touch at all since my mother died. I suppose he's pleased that the woman he hated for so long is finally dead.

No, Hollis is my main concern. Will he put all the pieces together and come for me? I guess there's only one way to find out.

"Hello!"

I'm not expecting anyone to know me. The voice jolts me from my thoughts. I see a woman with bleach-blonde hair waving at me, smiling.

"Hi," I reply.

"I remember you. You were going to North Yorkshire to meet your family," she says.

"That's right."

"Oh, hey, you weren't kidding about picking up accents. You sound like a native. So, you're going back to New York, then? How did it go? Was it weird seeing them again?"

"I did everything I wanted to do," I reply.

"Oh, great! Are you going back home now?"

"Yes," I say. "I'm going to live with my sister."

THE END

ABOUT THE AUTHOR

Sarah A. Denzil is a British suspense writer from Derbyshire. In her alternative life—AKA YA author Sarah Dalton—she writes speculative fiction for teenagers, including *The Blemished*, *Mary Hades* and *White Hart*.

Sarah lives in Yorkshire with her partner, enjoying the scenic countryside and rather unpredictable weather.

Saving April, Sarah's debut suspense thriller, is a psychological look into the minds of the people around us who we rarely even consider—our neighbours. What do we really know about them, and what goes on when the doors are closed?

https://www.facebook.com/sarahadenzil/
https://twitter.com/sarahdenzil
http://www.sarahdenzil.com/

Writing as Sarah Dalton -
http://www.sarahdaltonbooks.com/